Rainbow Edition

Reading Mastery I/II   Fast Cycle

Teacher's Guide

Siegfried Engelmann • Elaine C. Bruner

SRA

Macmillan/McGraw–Hill

Columbus, Ohio

SRA Macmillan/McGraw-Hill
250 Old Wilson Bridge Road
Suite 310
Worthington, Ohio 43085
Printed in the United States of America.
ISBN 0-02-686371-5
1 2 3 4 5 6 7 8 9 0 IPC 99 98 97 96 95 94

CONTENTS

Introduction

Reading Mastery: Fast Cycle I and II is an accelerated beginning-reading program for children of average or above-average ability. Fast Cycle provides a one-year first-grade program of 170 daily lessons. After completing Fast Cycle II, the children should go into a third-level reading program (ideally Reading Mastery III). In the third grade, they should be placed in a fourth-level program, and so forth, completing six years of reading instruction in only five years and being at least one year accelerated in skill development.

The Fast-Cycle program teaches all the word attack and the basic comprehension skills that are taught in Reading Mastery I and II, which is a two-year sequence.

Upon completing the program, children will read on a solid beginning-third-grade level because they will have mastered the first two years of reading skills in only one school year.

Program Materials

The following materials are for the teacher's use. They are included in the Fast-Cycle Kit.

- *Four Presentation Books.* These books specify each activity in each lesson and tell the teacher how to present it. Planning Pages appear every 20 lessons. These present an overview of skills taught, a summary of special considerations for upcoming lessons, and additional reading activities.

- *The Teacher's Guide.* The guide explains the program and provides instructions on how to teach it.
- *Two Storybooks.* These are copies of the story books that the children use.
- *A Teacher's Take-Home Book.* This is an annotated version of the children's take-home books.
- *The Spelling Book.* This book contains 79 spelling lessons, which begin at reading Lesson 36 and continue through Lesson 114.
- *A Behavioral Objectives Booklet.* This booklet lists specific objectives for each skill taught in the program.
- *One Skills Profile Folder.* This folder contains a summary of the skills taught in the program and provides a space for indicating when a child has mastered each skill. One folder is needed for each child.
- *An acetate page protector.* This overlay enables you to write on the pages of the presentation books when necessary.
- *A set of group progress indicators.* These clips enable you to keep track of the place each group has reached in the program.

Each child should have the following:

- *Two Storybooks* (one softbound and one hardbound). These nonconsumable books contain the stories for Lessons 44 to 170.
- *Four Take-Home Books.* These consumable workbooks contain written activities for every lesson.

Structure of the Program

The first eighty lessons of the program introduce all the skills that are presented in Reading Mastery I. The remaining ninety lessons present all the skills taught in Reading Mastery II.

The first nine lessons of the program introduce the prereading skills that are needed for the first word-reading exercises. These lessons teach children how to say words fast, how to sequence events, and how to identify a few letters as *sounds*.

Word reading begins in lesson 10 and continues in every lesson throughout the program. Initially, children sound out words before identifying them. Later (beginning with lesson 27) children learn to read words the fast way, without first sounding them out.

For the first 111 lessons of the program, words appear in the Distar orthography, or print. The system is designed to point out the regularities in words. The Distar orthography has joined letters (such as **th** and **sh**), long lines over long vowels (such as **ē**, which is pronounced as the ending sound in the word **me**), and small letters that are not to be pronounced (such as the a in the word **eₐt**.)

The Distar orthography is gradually faded: the joined letters become unjoined; the small letters become full-sized; and the lines over long vowels are removed. From lesson 112 to the end of the program, the children read words and stories written entirely in traditional print.

Comprehension skills are scheduled as part of each daily lesson. Children answer questions about what they read. They interpret pictures. They make predictions about what will happen in a story. And they perform on a variety of comprehension activities that are designed to shape their understanding of what they read and of how to read for understanding. For instance, children are presented with extensive practice in following written directions. By lesson 151 they independently read factual-information passages and answer questions. And the final sequence in the program is a fifteen-lesson story about a girl who goes to a very strange land. To leave the land, she must learn sixteen rules. The children discover these rules and apply them to the events described in the story.

Spelling is also part of the Fast-Cycle program. Material for 79 spelling lessons is provided for reading lessons 36 through 114. The recommendation for lessons 115 through 170 is to place students in Spelling Mastery Level A, which is a 60-lesson program.

A summary of decoding and comprehension skills taught in various lessons of the Fast-Cycle program appears on the next page.

Program Activities That Relate to Word Decoding

FAST CYCLE I			FAST CYCLE II
Prereading (Lessons 1-9)	**Sounding out words (Lessons 10-35)**	**Reading words the fast way (Lessons 36-170)**	**Word analysis (Lessons 81-170)**

Sound pronunciation
 	
Sequencing
 	
Oral blending
    Saying words slowly
    Saying words fast
 	
Rhyming
 	
Symbol identification (as sounds)
	Symbol identification
	
	Reading vocabulary (word lists)
		Symbol identification
		
		Reading vocabulary
		
		Decoding words in traditional print
			Symbol identification (sound combinations)
			
			Reading vocabulary
			    Word parts
			    Final-e words

	Story reading	Story reading Individual checkouts for rate and accuracy	
Independent workbook practice	Independent workbook practice	Independent workbook practice	Independent workbook practice

Program Activities That Relate to Comprehension

FAST CYCLE I		FAST CYCLE II
Prereading (Lessons 1-9)	**Beginning reading (Lessons 10-80)**	**Extended comprehension activities (Lessons 81-170)**
Sequencing events Picture comprehension	Comprehension of vocabulary words Story comprehension—oral Story comprehension—written Picture comprehension Comprehension games	Comprehension of vocabulary words Story comprehension—oral Story comprehension—written Picture comprehension Rule review Read the items Reading comprehension passages Following instructions Story-picture items Picture deductions Written deductions Factual information passages

Time Requirements for Reading

Lessons should be scheduled on every available school day. Ideally, children should be placed in small, homogeneous groups. Reading periods should allow at least forty minutes for teacher preparation and independent work. In addition, a daily ten-minute block should be available for spelling instruction.

The Lessons

No extensive lesson planning is necessary because each Fast-Cycle lesson provides all the information needed to present all activities of the lesson. The presentation book presents a detailed set of instructions for all activities. The instructions tell you what to do, what to say, and what children say when they respond appropriately to a task.

Although lesson planning is not necessary, preparation is. To present the activities in the lesson quickly and effectively—following program specifications—requires practice. Before presenting the program, make sure that you practice the tasks in the first lessons and that you can present these tasks smoothly, without "reading" every word from the script. As you work with the program every day, you will become familiar with the various tasks that are presented, and presenting from a script will become very natural. At first, however, it may seem highly unnatural.

Below is a task from the first lesson in the Fast-Cycle program. It shows the various conventions that are used in the teacher directions throughout the program. For this task, you show the presentation book to the children, touch the ball of the arrow at the bottom of the page, and present the activity. Note that the teacher instructions provide correction procedures for the more common mistakes the children might make.

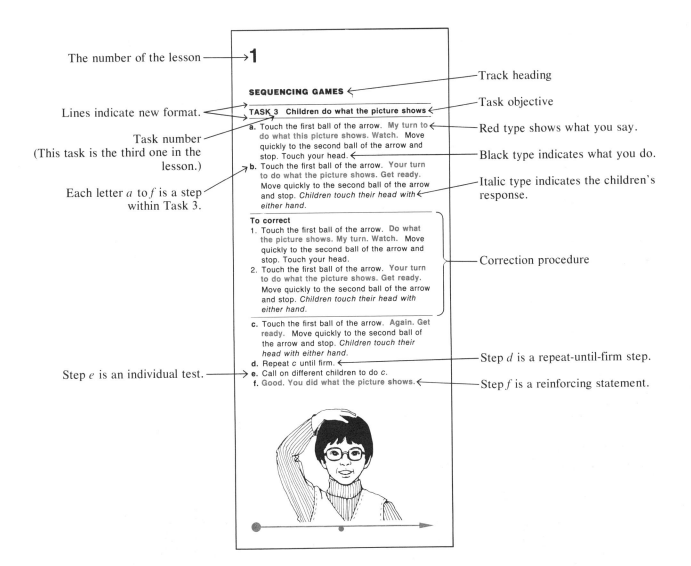

The number of the lesson

Lines indicate new format.

Task number
(This task is the third one in the
lesson.)

Each letter *a* to *f* is a step
within Task 3.

Step *e* is an individual test.

Track heading

Task objective

Red type shows what you say.

Black type indicates what you do.

Italic type indicates the children's
response.

Correction procedure

Step *d* is a repeat-until-firm step.

Step *f* is a reinforcing statement.

1

SEQUENCING GAMES

TASK 3   Children do what the picture shows

a. Touch the first ball of the arrow. My turn to
do what this picture shows. Watch. Move
quickly to the second ball of the arrow and
stop. Touch your head.

b. Touch the first ball of the arrow. Your turn
to do what the picture shows. Get ready.
Move quickly to the second ball of the arrow
and stop. *Children touch their head with
either hand.*

To correct
1. Touch the first ball of the arrow. Do what
the picture shows. My turn. Watch. Move
quickly to the second ball of the arrow and
stop. Touch your head.
2. Touch the first ball of the arrow. Your turn
to do what the picture shows. Get ready.
Move quickly to the second ball of the arrow
and stop. *Children touch their head with
either hand.*

c. Touch the first ball of the arrow. Again. Get
ready. Move quickly to the second ball of
the arrow and stop. *Children touch their
head with either hand.*
d. Repeat c until firm.
e. Call on different children to do c.
f. Good. You did what the picture shows.

How to Use the Presentation Books

The presentation books are divided into lessons. The number of the lesson appears at the top of every page. The first page of the lesson is indicated by the word **Lesson** preceding the number; the last page is indicated by the words **End of Lesson** at the bottom of the page.

In each lesson the track headings (such as Sounds, Say It Fast, or Sequencing Games) are printed in boldface capitals. The track titles tell you the skill developed in the tasks that follow. The tasks are numbered and the number is followed by a brief description of that task's objective.

What you are to **say** is in red type. What your are to **do** is in black type. The oral responses expected from the children are in italics. Expected motor responses are also in italics. Frequently, the children's response is followed by your repetition of the response as a reinforcement for the children. Each small letter (**a, b, c,** and so on) indicates a step in the task. Everything that you will say and do in teaching the task is specified in these steps.

Some task titles have lines above and below them. The lines signal the introduction of a new format.

Implementing the Program

Placement

Before you begin teaching the program, administer the placement test printed below to each child. Use the test to determine whether a child enters Reading Mastery I at lesson 1 or at lesson 11 or whether the child should enter Reading Mastery: Fast Cycle I. The test is scored on the Placement Test Scoring Sheet, which appears on page 96 of this book. Make one copy of this sheet for each child.

Administer the test individually to each child, circling the number of points earned for each task on a Placement Test Scoring Sheet. Then circle the appropriate entry point for the child. Testing each child requires about two to four minutes. You should be able to complete the testing of all the children within one hour on the first day of school. Instruction should begin on the second day.

PLACEMENT TEST

PART 1

Task 1   Total possible: 2 points

(Circle 1 point on the scoring sheet for each correct response at *b* and *c*.)

This is an oral task. For step *c,* say the sound **d,** not the letter name.
a. You're going to say some sounds.
b. (test item) Say (pause) **rrr.** *rrr.*
c. (test item) Now say (pause) **d.** *d.*

Task 2   Total possible: 10 points

(Circle 1 point on the scoring sheet for each correct response at *b*.)

a. Point to the sounds. **These are sounds.** Point to the boxed **m. This sound is** (pause) **mmm. What sound?** Touch **m.** *mmm.*
b. (test items) Point to each unboxed sound in the column. For each sound, ask: **Is this** (pause) **mmm?**

(Circle 1 point on the scoring sheet for each correct response at step *d*.)

c. Point to the boxed **a. This sound is** (pause) **ăăă. What sound?** Touch **a.** *ăăă.*
d. (test items) Point to each unboxed sound in the column. For each sound, ask: **Is this** (pause) **ăăă?**

Task 3   Total possible: 4 points

(Circle 2 points on the scoring sheet for each correct response at *b* and *c*.)

a. Let's play Say It Fast. Listen. **Ice** (pause) **box.** I can say it fast. **Icebox.**
b. (test item) Listen. **Foot** (pause) **ball.** (Pause.) Say it fast. *Football.* Yes, **football.**
c. (test item) Here's another word. Listen. (Pause.) **Nnnōōōzzz.** (Pause.) Say it fast. *Nose.* Yes, **nose.**

Task 4   Total possible: 4 points

(Circle 2 points on the scoring sheet for each correct response at *b* and *d*.)

This is an oral task. Do not stop between the sounds when saying zzzoooooo or wwwēēē.

a. First I'll say a word slowly. Then you'll say that word slowly. I'll say (pause) **zoo** slowly. Listen. (Pause.) **Zzzooooooo.**
b. (test item) Your turn. Say (pause) **zzzooooooo.** *Zzzooooooo.*
   (A child scores 2 points if he or she says the correct sounds without stopping between the sounds.)
c. Now I'll say (pause) **wē** slowly. Listen. (Pause.) **Wwwēēē.**
d. (test item) Your turn. Say (pause) **wwwēēē.**
   (A child scores 2 points if he or she says the correct sounds without stopping between the sounds.)

Add the number of points the child earned on part 1. Note: Administer part 2 **only** to children who made 19 or 20 points on part 1.

PART 2

Task 1   Total possible: 4 points

(Circle 2 points on the scoring sheet for each correct response at *a* and *b*.)

a. (test item) Point to the boxed **m.** Let's see if you remember this sound. (Pause.) What sound? Touch **m.** *mmm.*
b. (test item) Point to the boxed **a.** Let's see if you remember this sound. (Pause.) What sound? Touch **a.** *ăăă.*

Task 2   Total possible: 6 points

(Circle 1 point on the scoring sheet for each correct response at *b, c,* and *d*.)

a. I'll say a word slowly. Then I'll say it fast. Listen. (Pause.) **Mmmaaannn.** (Pause.) I can say it fast. **Man.**
b. (test item) Your turn. Say (pause) **iiinnn.** *iiinnn.*
   (test item) Say it fast. *In.*
c. (test item) Your turn. Say (pause) **aaat.** *Aaat.*
   (test item) Say it fast. *At.*
d. (test item) Your turn. Say (pause) **sssiiit.** *Sssiiit.*
   (test item) Say it fast. *Sit.*

End of Placement Test

Summary of Placement Information

Part 1 of the Placement Test

Children who made 0-14 points begin with Reading Mastery I, lesson 1.

Children who made 15-18 points begin with Reading Mastery I, lesson 11.

Children who made 19-20 points should proceed with Part 2 of the placement test.

Part 2 of the Placement Test

Children who made 0-7 points begin with Reading Mastery I, lesson 11.

Children who made 8-10 points should be placed, if possible, in Reading Mastery: Fast Cycle I.

Grouping

Here is a guide for grouping children according to their performance on the placement test:

1. Divide the class into no more than three groups.
2. Make the lowest-performing group the smallest and the highest-performing group the largest.

Testing Throughout the Year

Throughout Fast Cycle I, children are given mastery tests. The mastery tests are short. They generally test only one skill and are given after specified lessons in the program. There are nineteen tests in all. They appear in the presentation books at the point at which they are to be presented. The first test is presented after lesson 7.

The mastery tests give you feedback on the effectiveness of your teaching; they serve as a backup for your daily evaluation of the children's performance; and they provide information for regrouping the children at later points in the program.

Administering the Mastery Tests

Use the following procedures when administering the mastery tests.

1. Test each child individually.

2. No child should see or hear another child being tested before he or she has taken the test.

3. Test the children at a time other than during the regularly scheduled reading lesson. Your most capable children may be tested a day or two early, so that only the children you are doubtful about will have to be tested on the day indicated in the presentation book.

4. Before presenting a test, write the names of the children in the group on a sheet of paper. After presenting each test item, record a pass (P) or a fail (F) next to the child's name. At the end of the test, record the total number of items missed by the child.

5. When presenting the test, have the child sit next to you so that both of you can see and work from the test book.

6. Use the plastic page protector when doing the story-reading tests.

Regrouping

Any child who repeatedly fails items on the mastery tests should be placed in a lower reading group. Repeated failure indicates that the child cannot maintain the pace set by other members of the group. If a child is already in the lowest-performing group, try to work with the child individually. If there is a teacher using Reading Mastery I in your school, consider putting the low performers into a group and assigning them to that teacher. This will allow the children to move at a pace that is more appropriate for them and to receive the individual attention they need. It will also allow the groups from which they have been removed to progress at a faster rate.

On the other hand, if a child consistently performs better than most of the other children in a group, the child should be moved to a higher group. Plan to regroup the children at several points throughout the year. Suggested points for regrouping are after Mastery Test 1 (lesson 7), after Mastery Test 3 (lesson 20), and after Mastery Test 6 (lesson 36).

Group Performance

It is important to complete a lesson each day with each group. Occasionally, you may find that, if you firm the skill so that all children can perform, you will not be able to complete the entire lesson. When the choice is between firming all the children and completing the lesson, choose the firming. The best procedure is to *firm the children when new skills are first introduced.*

Presenting Reading Mastery Tasks

The remainder of this guide gives you instructions on how to teach Reading Mastery: Fast Cycle. Pages 9 and 10 specify general teaching strategies (how to seat the children, how to present signals so that the children respond together, and so forth). Following the general teaching strategies is a detailed description of the tasks in Fast Cycle I and how to present them. Next is a section on the tasks in Fast Cycle II.

Before teaching the program, study pages 11 through 21, the Prereading section of this guide, and practice each of the formats. Simply examining the tasks will not ensure that you will present them well; you must actually say the words, practice the signals, and practice the various corrections that are specified.

Children will make the mistakes indicated in the formats, and the corrections you practice will be needed.

Throughout the year, consult this teacher's guide for new formats that will be appearing in the program. Always practice new formats before the top group reaches them. In this way you will be reasonably well prepared for your top group, and by the time your lowest-performing group reaches the lesson in which the new format appears, you will be quite proficient at presenting it.

General Teaching Strategies

How to Set Up the Group

1. Seat the children in a semicircle in front of you. Sit so that you can observe every child in the group and the other members of the class who are engaged in independent work. Ideally, children in the group should sit on chairs, not at desks.

2. Test to see that all children can see the presentation book. Do this by holding your head next to the book and looking to see whether you can see the eyes of all the children. If you have to look almost sideways from the book to see a child's eyes, that child won't be able to see what is on the page.

3. Ideally, keep all children within touching distance. There will be times during the lesson when you will want to hand the presentation book to a child, or to reinforce a child. This will be easier if the children are all within arm's reach. Sit close to the children and group them close together.

4. Place the lowest performers directly in front of you (in the first row if there is more than one row). Seat the highest performers on the ends of the group (or in the second row). You will naturally look most frequently at the children seated directly in front of you. You should teach until each child is firm. When the lowest performers are firm, the rest of the group will be firm.

5. Seat the children so that cliques are broken. Assign the seats. The children should sit in their assigned seats each day. This will allow you to separate disruptive buddies and will allow you to learn which voices to listen to during the presentation.

Getting into the Lesson

1. On the day that you begin the program, introduce the rules that the group is to follow. Summarize the rules: "Sit tall, look at the book, and talk big." Note that these rules express precisely what the children are supposed to do. Reinforce the children for following the rules.

2. Get into the lesson *quickly*. If the group is shy or tends to present behavior problems, begin by telling the children "Stand up . . . Touch your nose . . ." until all of them are responding without hesitation. This establishes that you are directing what the children are to do. Then quickly present the first task. The same technique can be used if the children's attention lags during the presentation.

3. Present each task until the children are firm. If the first task is a say-it-fast task, do not move to the second task in the lesson until the children are firm.

4. Use clear signals. All signals have the same purpose: to trigger a simultaneous response from the group. All signals have the same rationale: if you can get the group to respond simultaneously (with no child leading the others) you will receive information about the performance of all the children, not just those who happen to answer first. While the children are working from examples in the presentation book, be sure to hold the book so that every child in the group can see it. When pointing to or touching examples in the book, do not cover anything that the children should see.

5. Pace tasks appropriately. Pacing is one of the more difficult presentational skills to master. Pacing is the rate at which different parts of the task are presented. Not all portions of a task should be presented at the same rate. Different pacing is specified throughout the guide. Many formats contain such instructions as, "Pause one second," or, "Pause three seconds."

6. Reinforce good performance. Make your praise specific. If the children have just completed a sounds page with no errors, reinforce them: "Wow! You know every sound on the page." If they have just said the sounds in **am** correctly, say, "Yes, **am**." Praise the children for following the rules. If they are all talking up, say, "Good talking. I can hear everybody." Do not reinforce yelling.

Teaching to Criterion

At the conclusion of any task, every child should be able to perform the task independently, without making mistakes. Children are "at criterion" or "firm" on a task only when they can perform quickly and confidently with the correct response. Your goal is to teach so that every child is at criterion.

Bring the children to criterion on the first introduction of a format. By firming children quickly, you guarantee that the children hear the correct responses the first time an exercise is presented.

Let the children know what your criterion is. Keep on a task until you can honestly say to them, "Terrific. Everybody read every word correctly." The stricter your criterion, the fewer the tasks your group will have to repeat after taking the mastery tests.

Individual Turns

Individual turns are specified in the tasks or under the heading **Individual Test**. Follow these rules when administering individual turns:

1. Present individual turns only after the group is firm. If you go to individual turns too soon, many children will not give firm responses. If you wait until the children are firm on group responses, the chances are much better that the children will not make mistakes on individual turns.

2. Give most of your individual turns to the lower-performing children in the group. If these children can perform the task without mistakes, the other children in the group will also be able to perform the task.

3. If you are in doubt about the performance of any children on tasks that do not have specified individual turns, present quick individual turns.

4. The following procedure is recommended for administering individual turns once group responses on a task are firm. First you can state: "Time for individual turns." Then *focus* on the task for students to think and practice. Finally, call on an individual student to respond to the task. This procedure helps to keep the entire group alert to you and practicing the task until a specific student's name is called.

Corrections

The major difference between the average teacher, who teaches *most* of the children, and the outstanding teacher, who teaches *all* of the children, is the ability to correct.

Information on general corrections appears below. Study the procedures and practice them until you can execute corrections immediately, without hesitation. Corrections must be automatic. Unacceptable behavior that calls for correction includes nonattending, nonresponding, signal violations, and response errors.

Nonattending. For example, if a child is not attending to the sound to which you are pointing, correct by looking at the nonattender and saying:

Watch my finger. Let's try it again. Return to the beginning of the task. Reinforce the children who are paying attention.

Nonresponding. This behavior occurs when a child fails to answer when you signal for a response. If a child is not responding, correct the child by saying:

I have to hear everybody. Return to the beginning of the task.

Signal Violations. A signal violation occurs when the child responds either before or after the other children respond. If children respond either early or late, you will not get information from every child. Remember that the purpose of a signal is to trigger a simultaneous group response. If you fail to enforce the signal, you will have to present many individual turns to find out which children are firm and which children are weak.

Correct signal-violation mistakes by telling the children what they did, repeating the signal, and then returning to the beginning of the task:

You're early, or You're late, or You didn't say it when I touched. Watch my finger. Get ready. Touch. The children respond as you touch. Now, let's try it again. Return to the beginning of the task.

If you are spending a lot of time correcting nonattending, nonresponding, and signal violations, your pacing is probably too slow or your pacing of the signal inconsistent. The object of a signal is not to keep the children sitting on the edges of their seats, never knowing when they will have to respond next. The pacing of the signal should be perfectly predictable so the children know when to respond.

Response Errors. A response error is a mistake. If you touch the sound **a** and the children say *mmm*, they make a response error. The corrections that appear in the program generally follow these steps:

1. You tell the correct answer.
2. You repeat the question or the instructions that signal the response.
3. You present a *delayed test*. For this test, you repeat part of the activity before presenting the item on which the mistake occurred. The delayed test lets you know that the correction was successfully communicated to the children.

Fast Cycle I
(Lessons 1–80)

PREREADING

At lesson 10 the children begin to read words. Lessons 1 to 9 are designed to set the stage for word reading. The activities presented in this part of the program are possibly the most important in the entire program. If children master these activities, they typically have little trouble with the next instructional steps. However, if children are not taught these prereading skills, they will probably have serious trouble throughout the program.

During these beginning lessons, the children learn to identify symbols as "sounds"; they practice sequencing events—*first* and *next* events; they firm their oral-blending skills by saying words slowly and saying them fast; and they learn to rhyme. Rhyming provides children with a basis for seeing how words that have parts that look the same have parts that sound the same.

General Teaching Strategies

The following section of this guide is designed to help you practice the specific skills that you will use when working with children. The section explains the purpose of each track in the prereading section. It presents some of the key formats, or exercises, within the track. It also indicates how to correct some of the more common mistakes the children will make.

The best way to learn the skills that are required is to practice, and the best way to practice is with a partner. During the initial practice sessions, you and your partner should take turns playing the roles of teacher and child. The "child" should respond correctly to all tasks and should give the "teacher" feedback about how the teacher executed the different parts of the format.

After you are able to run the format smoothly, practice the format with corrections. Practice correcting mistakes the children are most likely to make. Anticipate that you will have to use each of these corrections.

Sounds (Lessons 1–89)

In Fast-Cycle, children are initially taught to decode words by sounding them out. To sound out a word successfully, the children must be firm in sounds identification. Sounds activities, therefore, appear in every lesson through lesson 89. The two primary formats in the Sounds track are a *sound-introduction* format, used to introduce and reinforce each new sound, and a *sound-firming* format, in which several sounds are reviewed and firmed up. Other formats include game formats, such as a cross-out game, a child-plays-teacher game, and a sounds game. Letters are referred to as *sounds* in Fast Cycle I. Alphabet names are taught in Fast Cycle II.

Throughout most of Fast Cycle I, each symbol stands for a single sound. The symbol **a** stands for the sound **aaa** (as in **and**). It does not stand for **a** as in **ate**, in **all**, or in **father**.

To allow the children to read more words as "regular words," four conventions are followed in the program:

1. Some sounds are represented by joined letters: **th**, **ch**, **sh**, **wh**, **qu**, **er**, **oo**, and **i͡ng**.

2. Macrons (long lines over vowels) appear over long vowels. For example, the symbol **ā** makes the long vowel sound in **āte**.

3. Some symbols are altered to reduce some of the confusion children typically have between pairs of letters that appear very much alike in traditional orthography. For example:

$$\mathbf{b\ d \qquad h\ n \qquad f\ t \qquad J\ i}$$

4. Only lowercase letters are taught in Fast Cycle I.

By the middle of Fast Cycle II, all letters are printed in traditional orthography and the capital letters have been taught.

The children are taught forty sounds. Initially only one value is taught for each sound. New sounds are introduced about every two or three lessons. A list of the lessons in which new sounds are introduced appears on the last page of this guide. Note that the children start to read words at lesson 10, after six sounds have been introduced (**a, m, s, ē, r,** and **d**).

Before teaching the program, practice pronouncing the sounds that appear on the pronunciation chart on the last page of this guide.

Note that some sounds are continuous sounds and some are stop sounds. Continuous sounds can be held until you run out of breath. Continuous sounds include all vowels and **s, m, r, l, th,** and **sh**. Stop sounds are sounds that must be produced very quickly, like **d, b, c, g, h, p, t**.

The first sounds taught in the program are continuous sounds because they are easier for the children to pronounce.

Continuous-Sound Signal

All signals follow the same basic rules:

- You talk first; then signal.
- You never signal when talking.
- You always pause the same length of time between the end of your talking and the signal for the children to respond—about one second.

Remember, talk first, then signal, and keep the timing the same for every signal. Think of a signal as something like a dance step. If it's done right and in time, your partner can follow. If the timing is off, somebody's going to stumble.

To signal children to respond to a continuous sound, follow these steps:

1. Touch the first ball of the arrow.
2. Keep your finger on that ball as you say, "Get ready."
3. Pause for one second. Then move quickly to the ball under **a** and hold on that ball for two seconds. As soon as you touch that ball, *all* the chilren are to respond.

Practice touching the first ball, saying, "Get ready," pausing one second, and then moving quickly to the second ball and holding your finger there for two seconds.

Continuous-Sounds Teaching Techniques

Practice the following sounds-introduction format from lesson 1 after you are very consistent with your signal. Note that the last thing you say before signaling is always, "Get ready." Timing is the same as it is for the simple signal that you practiced. Pause after saying "Get ready" and move quickly to the second ball. Hold at the second ball as either you or the children respond. The letters **aaa** in the teacher's script remind you to hold the sound.

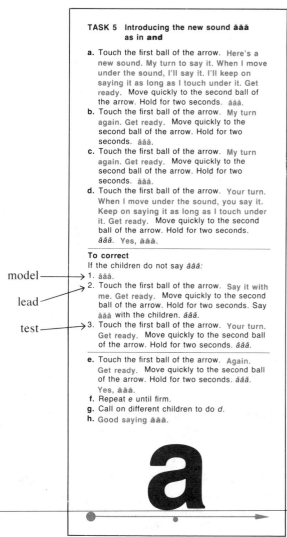

Lesson 1

- Steps *a* through *c* model the behavior so the children know *what* they should respond and *how* they should respond in steps *d* and *e.*.
- Step *d* is the first time the students are to respond.
- Following step *d* is a correction to be used if the children respond incorrectly. Present the correction *as soon as* you hear or see any child responding incorrectly. The correction steps have been labeled to help you see the model-lead-test procedure. For the lead step, you respond with the children.
- Step *f* directs you to repeat step *e* until firm. "Firm" means that all children are responding clearly as soon as you touch under the sound and that all children are saying the sound as long as you touch under it.
- At step *g* you call on different children to identify the sound.

Stop-Sound Signal

The sound **d** above is a stop sound, a sound that cannot be held for more than an instant without distorting it. The following procedures are used to signal for stop sounds:

- Touch the ball of the arrow.
- Say, **Say it fast.**
- Pause for one second.
- Quickly move your finger to the end of the arrow. As you pass under the arrowhead that is directly under the **d**, the children are to say the sound, *d* (not *duh* or *dih*—simply *d*).

Note that the signal for the stop sound involves the same timing as the signal for the continuous sound. The only difference is that you don't stop under the sound; you just keep moving to the end of the arrow.

If you have trouble pronouncing a stop sound, say a word that ends in the sound. Say the sound in an exaggerated manner. That is the way you would pronounce the sound when teaching the children to identify the symbol. For instance, say the word **sad**, exaggerating the **d**. Be careful not to say **saduh**.

Stop-Sounds Teaching Techniques

In the teacher's script and on the pronunciation chart, stop sounds are represented by a single letter, such as **d**, **t**, or **c**, to help you remember to say the sound fast. This compares with the three letters (**aaa**) used to remind you to hold continuous sounds. After you practice the basic signal for stop sounds, practice the following sounds-introduction format.

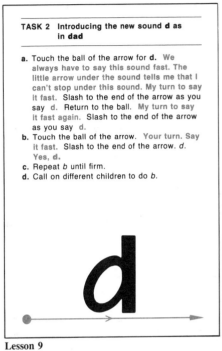

> **TASK 2   Introducing the new sound d as in dad**
>
> a. Touch the ball of the arrow for **d.** We always have to say this sound fast. The little arrow under the sound tells me that I can't stop under this sound. My turn to say it fast. Slash to the end of the arrow as you say **d.** Return to the ball. My turn to say it fast again. Slash to the end of the arrow as you say *d.*
> b. Touch the ball of the arrow. Your turn. Say it fast. Slash to the end of the arrow. *d.* Yes, *d.*
> c. Repeat *b* until firm.
> d. Call on different children to do *b*.

Lesson 9

In step *b*, pause after you say, "Your turn," and before you say, "Say it fast," to give the children a moment to think.

Correction

If students mispronounce the sound at step *b*, correct as follows:

1. (*Model*) Say, d.
2. (*Test*) Touch the ball of the arrow. Say, Your turn. Say it fast. Slash to the end of the arrow. Children say, *d.*

Sounds Firm-Up Teaching Techniques

In sounds-firm-up tasks, the children review and practice sounds they have learned. Sounds-firm-up tasks appear in every lesson starting with lesson 2. Firm-up tasks are the most important source of feedback about how well the children have learned sounds. There are no new signals in the tasks. Use the signals that you have already practiced for continuous sounds and stop sounds.

TASK 3 Sounds firm-up

a. Point to the sounds in the columns. **Get ready to tell me all these sounds.** Remember, if a sound has a little arrow under it, you have to say it fast. Don't get fooled.

b. Touch the first ball of the arrow for **r.** (Pause one second.) **Get ready.** Move quickly to the second ball. Hold. *rrr.* **Yes, *rrr.***

c. Repeat *b* for each remaining sound. For **d,** slash to the end of the arrow.

d. Repeat *b* and *c* until all children are firm on all sounds.

e. Call on different children to say all the sounds.

f. Good. You said all the sounds.

r
ē
d

Lesson 9

Step *e* of the format calls for individual children to say all the sounds in the column. The individual test is very important. You will receive feedback about how well each child has learned the sounds. Make sure that you give turns to the lower-performing children.

Correction

No correction box is in the task. If any child in the group misidentifies the sound at step *b*, correct as follows:

1. (*Model*) Say, *rrr.*
2. (*Test*) Touch the first ball of the arrow for **r.** Pause one second. Say, **Everybody, get ready.** Move to the second ball. Hold. Children say, *rrr.*

The following dialogue illustrates how to handle mistakes on individual turns. The teacher presents an individual turn to Lucy, who makes a mistake at step 4. The teacher corrects *the group,* and then returns to Lucy. This procedure is important. If an individual child makes a mistake, assume that others in the group would make the same mistake. By first correcting the group, you save time because you won't have to present the same correction to other members of the group. Read the dialogue out loud.

Script for Step e

1. Teacher: Touch the first ball of the arrow for **r.** **Lucy, your turn to say all the sounds in this column.** (Pause one second.) **Get ready.** Move quickly to the second ball. Hold.
2. Lucy: *rrr.*
3. Teacher: Yes, *rrr.* Touch the first ball of the arrow for **ē.** (Pause one second.) **Get ready.** Move quickly to the second ball. Hold.
4. Lucy: *aaa.*
5. Teacher: *ēēē.* Return to the first ball of the arrow for **ē.** (Pause one second.) **Everybody, get ready.** Move quickly to the second ball. Hold.
6. Group: *ēēē.*
7. Teacher: Yes, *ēēē.* Return to the first ball of the arrow of the arrow for **ē.** (Pause one second.) **Lucy, get ready.** Move quickly to the second ball. Hold.
8. Lucy: *ēēē.*
9. Teacher: Yes, *ēēē.* Return to the top of the column. Touch the first ball of the arrow for **r.** **Starting over.** (Pause one second.) **Lucy, get ready.** Move quickly to the second ball. Hold.
10. Lucy: *rrr.*
11. Teacher: Yes, *rrr.* Touch the first ball of the arrow for **ē.** (Pause one second.) **Get ready.** Move quickly to the second ball. Hold.
12. Lucy: *ēēē.*
13. Teacher: Yes, *ēēē.* Touch the ball of the arrow for **d.** (Pause one second.) **Get ready.** Slash to the end of the arrow.
14. Lucy: *d.*
15. Teacher: Yes, *d.* **Good. You said all the sounds in the column.**

Pronunciation (Lessons 1–21)

Purpose of the Track

This track provides practice in pronouncing sounds. All pronunciation exercises are oral. The children practice saying a sound before they identify the written symbol for that sound. The sounds that are practiced include those that may be difficult to pronounce. Pronunciation exercises precede sounds exercises, and always include any new sounds that will be introduced in that lesson.

Pronunciation Signal

To signal a sound response, hold up one finger. This signal will be used in several other tracks, including those oral tracks in which students say words or word parts slowly.

TASK 1 Children say the sounds

a. You're going to say some sounds. When I hold up my finger, say (pause) **d.** Get ready. Hold up one finger. *d.*

b. Next sound. Say (pause) **ŏŏŏ.** Get ready. Hold up one finger. *ŏŏŏ.*

c. Next sound. Say (pause) **fff.** Get ready. Hold up one finger. *fff.*

d. Repeat *c* for sounds **d, ŏŏŏ,** and **fff.**

e. Call on different children to do *a, b,* or *c.*

f. Good saying the sounds.

Lesson 2

Note that only in this oral task are short vowels written as **ŏŏŏ** or **ăăă.**

Pronunciation Teaching Techniques

• Signal so that continuous sounds like **ŏŏŏ** or **fff** are held for about two seconds, and stop sounds such as **d** are said fast.

• Make sure that the children are pronouncing the sounds correctly.

• When presenting a sound, remember to pause when saying, "Say (pause) d."

• Remember to present step *d* for each sound.

Correction

Correct mistakes by presenting a model, a lead, and then a test.

1. (*Model*) **Listen,** *ŏŏŏ.*
2. (*Lead*) **Say it with me. Get ready.** Hold up one finger. *ŏŏŏ.* **Again. Get ready.** Hold up one finger. *ŏŏŏ.*
3. (*Test*) **Your turn. Get ready.** Hold up one finger. The children say *ŏŏŏ.*

Sequencing Games (Lessons 1–3)

The sequencing games give the children practice in using the same "code" for sequencing events that they use in reading words. Written words contain letters that stand for sounds. The sounds are to be produced in order, from left to right. The sequencing games present the same left-to-right code. The difference is that the events to be sequenced are not letters or sounds, but actions that are pictured on the arrow.

The sequencing games teach students to respond to the words *first* and *next*. These words will be used on worksheet activities, in sequencing word parts, in sounding out, in word reading, and in sentence reading.

The sequencing games are highly reinforcing to the children and easy for you to correct. They use the

same starting ball, balls under the pictures, and arrows that will later appear when word reading is introduced.

TASK 3 Children do **first** and **next**

a. Touch the first ball of the arrow. First you'll do what it shows on the arrow. Then we'll see if you can do it without looking at the picture. My turn. Watch. Move quickly to the second ball and stop. This is what you do <u>first</u>. Open your mouth. Show me what you do <u>first</u>. Tap the second ball. *Children open their mouth.* Watch. Move quickly to the third ball and stop. This is what you do <u>next</u>. Touch your nose. Show me what you do <u>next</u>. Tap the third ball. *Children touch their nose.*

b. Touch the first ball of the arrow. Let's do it again. Show me what you're going to do <u>first</u>. Move quickly to the second ball and stop. *Children open their mouth.* Show me what you're going to do <u>next</u>. Move quickly to the third ball and stop. *Children touch their nose.*

c. Repeat *b* until firm.

d. Do not show the pictures. Let's see if you remember what you did <u>first</u> and what you did <u>next</u>. Show me what you did <u>first</u>. Get ready. (Signal.) *Children open their mouth.* Show me what you did <u>next</u>. Get ready. (Signal.) *Children touch their nose.*

e. Repeat *d* until firm.

f. Call on different children to do *d.*

Lesson 2

• Practice step *a* several times. Coordinate your lines with the various motor activities called for. Place the book on a table or use the teacher box as an easel.

• At steps *a* and *b*, tap the ball under the picture to signal the children to respond.

• At steps *d* and *f*, turn the book so that the children cannot see the page. To signal, hold up a finger or use a hand-drop signal. (See page 16.)

Corrections

If children make a mistake at step *b*, model. Touch under the appropriate ball of the arrow. **This is what you do first.** Open your mouth. **Show me what you do first.** Tap the ball. Or, **This is what you do next.** Touch your nose. **Show me what you do next.** Tap the ball.

The children should not have difficulties at steps *d* and *f* if you repeat step *b* until the children are firm.

Blending

The children start to read words, such as **me** and **am**, in lesson 10. The initial strategy the children are taught is to first sound out the word, and then say it fast. This operation involves many skills. The children must be able to identify the symbols in the word. The children must understand that the written word presents a left-to-right code for sequencing the sounds. Finally, the children must be able to say the sounds of the word slowly and then say the sounds fast. These skills (saying words slowly and saying them fast) are blending skills. When we remove them from the context of word reading, they are oral activities. Oral-blending activities begin in lesson 1 and continue through the prereading lessons.

Say It Fast (Lessons 1–6)

Say-It-Fast Signal

- Hold out your hand as if you were stopping traffic.
- Keep it perfectly still.
- After saying "Say it fast," wait one second; then drop your hand quickly.
- The interval between "Say it fast" and the hand drop must be one second.

Hand-drop Signal

Say-It-Fast Teaching Techniques

The children-say-the-word-fast format is simple and easy to present after you have mastered the signal.

- In steps *b* and *c*, hold your hand steady.
- Say the word slowly in a monotone, without inflection.
- The children respond as soon as your hand drops.
- Always repeat the word ("Yes, **running**") to reinforce the correct response.
- Reinforce the children after they have responded correctly by saying, "Good. You said it fast."

When saying short words (for example, **ram** or **me**) say each sound slowly without pausing between the sounds. A good way to tell whether you are saying the sounds without stopping between them is to say the word **man** very slowly with your hand on your throat. If you are saying the sounds without stopping, you will feel a constant vibration of your throat as you say the word.

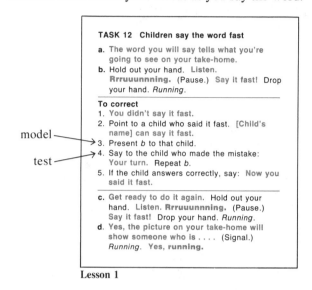

TASK 12   Children say the word fast

a. The word you will say tells what you're going to see on your take-home.

b. Hold out your hand. Listen. **Rrruuunnning.** (Pause.) Say it fast! Drop your hand. *Running.*

To correct
1. You didn't say it fast.
2. Point to a child who said it fast. [Child's name] can say it fast.
model → 3. Present *b* to that child.
test → 4. Say to the child who made the mistake: Your turn. Repeat *b*.
5. If the child answers correctly, say: Now you said it fast.

c. Get ready to do it again. Hold out your hand. Listen. **Rrruuunnning.** (Pause.) Say it fast! Drop your hand. *Running.*

d. Yes, the picture on your take-home will show someone who is . . . . (Signal.) *Running.* Yes, **running.**

Lesson 1

Say the Sounds (Lessons 1–2)

Activities in this track provide practice in *oral* sounding out. Children do not say the words fast.

Say-the-Sounds Signal

The signal for any sound said slowly is the same as you practiced in the Pronunciation track. For the word **fffuuunnn**, you hold up one finger for the **fff**, a second finger for the **uuu**, and a third finger for the **nnn**. Practice saying **fffuuunnn**, holding up a finger for each sound.

To help you hold each continuous sound for two seconds, you may want to tap your foot two beats for each sound.

The activity below is from the first say-the-sounds format in the program.

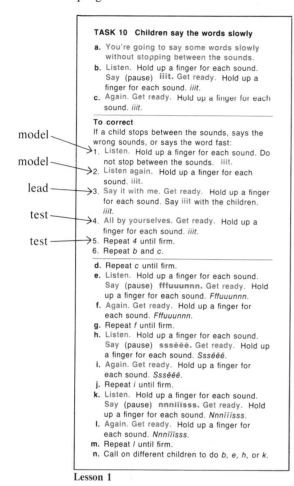

model →
model →
lead →
test →
test →

TASK 10 Children say the words slowly

a. You're going to say some words slowly without stopping between the sounds.
b. Listen. Hold up a finger for each sound. Say (pause) **iiit**. Get ready. Hold up a finger for each sound. *iiit*.
c. Again. Get ready. Hold up a finger for each sound. *iiit*.

To correct
If a child stops between the sounds, says the wrong sounds, or says the word fast:
1. Listen. Hold up a finger for each sound. Do not stop between the sounds. *iiit*.
2. Listen again. Hold up a finger for each sound. *iiit*.
3. Say it with me. Get ready. Hold up a finger for each sound. Say iiit with the children. *iiit*.
4. All by yourselves. Get ready. Hold up a finger for each sound. *iiit*.
5. Repeat 4 until firm.
6. Repeat b and c.

d. Repeat c until firm.
e. Listen. Hold up a finger for each sound. Say (pause) **ffuuunnn**. Get ready. Hold up a finger for each sound. *Fffuuunnn*.
f. Again. Get ready. Hold up a finger for each sound. *Fffuuunnn*.
g. Repeat f until firm.
h. Listen. Hold up a finger for each sound. Say (pause) **sssēēē**. Get ready. Hold up a finger for each sound. *Sssēēē*.
i. Again. Get ready. Hold up a finger for each sound. *Sssēēē*.
j. Repeat i until firm.
k. Listen. Hold up a finger for each sound. Say (pause) **nnniiisss**. Get ready. Hold up a finger for each sound. *Nnnīīīsss*.
l. Again. Get ready. Hold up a finger for each sound. *Nnnīīīsss*.
m. Repeat l until firm.
n. Call on different children to do b, e, h, or k.

Lesson 1

Say the Sounds—Say It Fast (Lessons 1–16)

This track consolidates the skills of saying words fast (taught in the Say It Fast track) and saying words slowly (taught in the Say the Sounds track).

Say-the-Sounds—Say-It-Fast Signals

Use two signals that you have already practiced—holding up one finger for each sound; then dropping your hand to signal **say it fast**.

Practice steps *a* through *f* with another adult making no mistakes.

TASK 5 Children say a word or sound slowly, then say it fast

a. I'm going to say some words and some sounds. First you're going to say them slowly. Then you're going to say them fast.
b. Listen. Hold up a finger for each sound. Say (pause) **rrroooc**. Get ready. Hold up a finger for each sound. *Rrroooc*. Again. Get ready. Hold up a finger for each sound. *Rrroooc*. Say it fast. (Signal.) *Rock*. Yes, **rock**.
c. Listen. Hold up one finger. Say (pause) **aaa**. Get ready. Hold up one finger. *aaa*. Again. Get ready. Hold up one finger. *aaa*. Say it fast. (Signal.) *a*. Yes, **a**.
d. Listen. Hold up a finger for each sound. Say (pause) **iiifff**. Get ready. Hold up a finger for each sound. *Iiifff*. Again. Get ready. Hold up a finger for each sound. *Iiifff*. Say it fast. (Signal.) *If*. Yes, **if**.
e. Repeat b through d until firm.
f. Call on different children to do b, c, or d.

Lesson 2

Sounds—Say It Fast (Lessons 2–8)

When children sound out words, they first say the parts slowly; then they say them fast. A simple variation of this procedure is to say a *single sound* slowly and then say it fast. For the exercises in this track, the children respond to written symbols.

Sounds—Say-It-Fast Signals

In the Sounds track you practiced two signals, one signal for saying a sound slowly (*aaa*) and one signal for saying a sound fast (*d*). (See pages 12 and 13.) You will use both these signals in steps *a* and *b* of the first format on page 18 as you model how to say a sound slowly, and then say it fast.

Fast Cycle I   17

Sounds—Say-It-Fast Teaching Techniques

Practice steps *a* and *b*. Remember to return to the first ball for a sound before you slash along the arrow to signal *say it fast*.

Steps *c* through *g* are tests in which the children first say a sound slowly, and then say the same sound fast.

Practice steps *a* through *g* with your partner making no mistakes.

TASK 10   Children say a sound slowly, then say it fast

a. Touch the first ball of the arrow for **a**. First we're going to say this sound slowly. Then we're going to say it fast. My turn to say it slowly. Get ready. Move quickly to the second ball. Hold for two seconds. **aaaaaa**. Return to the first ball. My turn to say it fast. Slash to the end of the arrow. **a**.

b. Touch the first ball of the arrow for **m**. My turn to say it slowly. Get ready. Move quickly to the second ball. Hold for two seconds. **mmmmmm**. Return to the first ball. My turn to say it fast. Slash to the end of the arrow. **m**.

c. Touch the first ball of the arrow for **a**. Your turn. Say the sound slowly. Get ready. Move quickly to the second ball. Hold for two seconds. *aaaaaa*. Return to the first ball. Say it fast. Slash to the end of the arrow. *a*. Yes, **a**.

d. Repeat *c* until firm.

e. Touch the first ball for **m**. Say the sound slowly. Get ready. Move to the second ball. Hold for two seconds. *mmmmmm*. Return to the first ball. Say it fast. Slash to the end of the arrow. *m*. Yes, **m**.

f. Repeat *e* until firm.

g. Call on different children to do *c* or *e*.

Lesson 2

Correction

If a child makes a mistake, present a model (step *a* or *b*) to the group; then test the group or child.

Say It Fast—Rhyming (Lessons 3–7)

This track is very important because it gives the children practice in blending words when the parts are presented *with a pause between them*. If the children are facile at rhyming, they have a much easier time reading words that begin with stop sounds (such as **bat** or **can**). Say-it-fast—rhyming gives the children practice in combining beginning sounds with endings. Also, if children later have trouble sounding out a word and happen to pause between the sounds, they will be in a better position to blend the word if they have received practice in handling two-part words.

Say-It-Fast—Rhyming Signal

Hold up one finger for the first sound and a second finger for the remainder of the word. When presenting the word **mat**, hold up one finger for the **mmm**, and one finger for **aaat**.

TASK 10   Children say word parts slowly, then say them fast

a. Here's a new Say it Fast. It's hard. Listen. Hold up one finger. First you'll say (pause) **mmm**. Hold up two fingers. Then you'll say (pause) **aaat**. Listen again. Hold up one finger. First you'll say (pause) **mmm**. Hold up two fingers. Then you'll say (pause) **aaat**.

b. My turn. Hold up one finger. Say **mmm**. Hold up two fingers. Without pausing, say **mmmaaat**.

c. Your turn to say it slowly. Get ready. Hold up one finger. *mmm*. Hold up two fingers. *Mmmaaat*.

d. Again. Say it slowly. Get ready. Hold up one finger. *mmm*. Hold up two fingers. *Mmmaaat*. Say it fast. (Signal.) *Mat*. Yes, **mat**.

e. Repeat *a* through *d* until firm.

f. Here's a new word. Listen. Hold up one finger. First you'll say (pause) **zzz**. Hold up two fingers. Then you'll say (pause) **oooooo**. Listen again. Hold up one finger. First you'll say (pause) **zzz**. Hold up two fingers. Then you'll say (pause) **oooooo**.

g. My turn. Hold up one finger. Say **zzz**. Hold up two fingers. Without pausing, say **zzzooooooo**.

h. Your turn to say it slowly. Get ready. Hold up one finger. *zzz*. Hold up two fingers. *Zzzooooooo*.

i. Again. Say it slowly. Get ready. Hold up one finger. *zzz*. Hold up two fingers. *Zzzooooooo*. Say it fast. (Signal.) *Zoo*. Yes, **zoo**.

j. Repeat *f* through *i* until firm.

k. Here's a new word. Listen. Hold up one finger. First you'll say (pause) **rrr**. Hold up two fingers. Then you'll say (pause) **uuunnn**. Listen again. Hold up one finger. First you'll say (pause) **rrr**. Hold up two fingers. Then you'll say (pause) **uuunnn**.

l. My turn. Hold up one finger. Say **rrr**. Hold up two fingers. Without pausing, say **rrruuunnn**.

m. Your turn to say it slowly. Get ready. Hold up one finger. *rrr*. Hold up two fingers. *Rrruuunnn*.

n. Again. Say it slowly. Get ready. Hold up one finger. *rrr*. Hold up two fingers. *Rrruuunnn*. Say it fast. (Signal.) *Run*. Yes, **run**.

o. Repeat *k* through *n* until firm.

p. Call on different children to do *a–d*, *f–i*, or *k–n*.

Lesson 3

Say-It-Fast—Rhyming Teaching Techniques

• Practice steps *a* and *b* until you can present them quite fast.

- In step *b*, do not say **mmm...mmmaaat**. The directions in the format simply tell you to continue saying the word as you hold up the second finger. Do not pause between the sounds.

mmmmmmmmmmmmmmmmmmmmmaaaaaaaaat
(one finger)   (two fingers)

- It helps if you sing the word, with both parts presented on the same note. By singing the word, you give the children a stronger cue for remembering its parts.

Correction

If the children make mistakes at step *c*, repeat your model, step *b*. Then present step *c* (a test).

Rhyming (Lessons 8–15)

The children "read" a sound such as *mmm* and say an ending such as *at*. Then they put the parts together and say it fast—*mat*. The difference between the activities in this track and those in the Say It Fast—Rhyming track is that, in this track, children are not *told* the first sound of the word; they "read" it from the presentation book. Then they combine it with a specified ending.

TASK 7   Children rhyme with un

a. Touch the first ball of the arrow for **r**. When I move under the sound, you say it. Get ready. Move quickly to the second ball. Hold. *rrr.* **Yes, rrr.**
b. You're going to rhyme with (pause) **uuunnn.** Hold up one finger. First you'll say **rrr.** Hold up two fingers. Then you'll say **uuunnn.**
c. Hold up one finger. What are you going to say first? (Signal.) *rrr.* Hold up two fingers. What are you going to say next? (Signal.) *Uuunnn.*
d. Repeat *c* until firm.
e. Return to the first ball. Do it with me. Rhyme with (pause) **uuunnn.** Get ready. Move quickly to the second ball. Hold. Say **rrr** with the children. *rrr.* Slash to the end of the arrow. Say **rrruuunnn** with the children. *Rrruuunnn.*
f. Repeat *e* until firm.
g. Return to the first ball. Your turn. Get ready. Move quickly to the second ball. Hold. *rrr.* Slash to the end of the arrow. *Rrruuunnn.*
h. Repeat *g* until firm.
i. Return to the first ball. Say it fast. Slash to the end of the arrow. *Run.* **Yes, run.**
j. Call on different children to do *g* and *i*.

Lesson 8

Other Rhyming Formats

In later rhyming formats, the children use different beginning sounds to create words that rhyme with a specified ending (**fan, ran**). In the last rhyming format, the children rhyme by first using a continuous-sound beginning, and then using a stop-sound beginning (**rim, dim**).

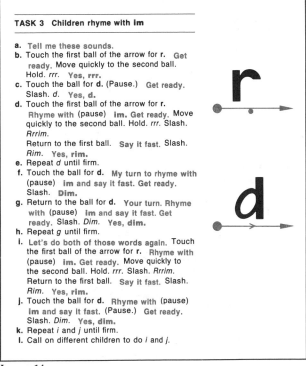

TASK 3   Children rhyme with im

a. Tell me these sounds.
b. Touch the first ball of the arrow for **r.** Get ready. Move quickly to the second ball. Hold. *rrr.* **Yes, rrr.**
c. Touch the ball for **d.** (Pause.) Get ready. Slash. *d.* **Yes, d.**
d. Touch the first ball of the arrow for **r.** Rhyme with (pause) **im.** Get ready. Move quickly to the second ball. Hold. *rrr.* Slash. *Rrrim.* Return to the first ball. Say it fast. Slash. *Rim.* **Yes, rim.**
e. Repeat *d* until firm.
f. Touch the ball for **d.** My turn to rhyme with (pause) **im** and say it fast. Get ready. Slash. **Dim.**
g. Return to the ball for **d.** Your turn. Rhyme with (pause) **im** and say it fast. Get ready. Slash. *Dim.* **Yes, dim.**
h. Repeat *g* until firm.
i. Let's do both of those words again. Touch the first ball of the arrow for **r.** Rhyme with (pause) **im.** Get ready. Move quickly to the second ball. Hold. *rrr.* Slash. *Rrrim.* Return to the first ball. Say it fast. Slash. *Rim.* **Yes, rim.**
j. Touch the ball for **d.** Rhyme with (pause) **im** and say it fast. (Pause.) Get ready. Slash. *Dim.* **Yes, dim.**
k. Repeat *i* and *j* until firm.
l. Call on different children to do *i* and *j*.

Lesson 14

Sound Out (Lessons 4–12)

The final prereading track is Sound Out. The activities in this track are similar to those in the Say the Sounds track, with one difference. In say-the-sounds exercises, the children repeat the sounds that the teacher says. In sound-out exercises, the children "read" the sounds.

The sounding-out skill is very important for initial word reading. And the most important part of this skill is saying the sounds of the word *without pausing or stopping between the sounds.* It is much easier to identify the word if the sounded-out word sounds like the word that is said at a normal speaking rate.

Sound-Out Signal

The illustration below shows you how to move on the arrow.

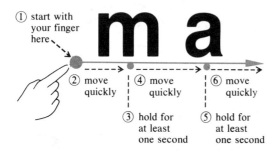

① start with your finger here
② move quickly
③ hold for at least one second
④ move quickly
⑤ hold for at least one second
⑥ move quickly

Practice the signal for step *a* without saying your lines. Become firm on the motor behaviors before you present the task to your partner. Start on the first ball of the arrow. Move quickly along the arrow, stopping for at least one second at each ball. After you have stopped at the last ball, you may either lift your finger from the page or move quickly to the end of the arrow.

TASK 7   Children say the sounds without stopping

a. Touch the first ball of the arrow for **sa**. My turn. I'll show you how to say these sounds without stopping between the sounds. Move under each sound. Hold. Say **sssaaa.**

b. Return to the first ball of the arrow for **sa**. Your turn. Say the sounds as I touch under them. Don't stop between the sounds. Get ready. Move under each sound. Hold. *Sssaaa.*
Return to the first ball of the arrow. Again. Get ready. Move under each sound. Hold. *Sssaaaa.*
Good saying **sssaaa.**

c. Touch the first ball of the arrow for **ma**. My turn. I'll show you how to say these sounds without stopping between the sounds. Move under each sound. Hold. Say **mmmaaa.**

d. Return to the first ball of the arrow for **ma**. Your turn. Say the sounds as I touch under them. Don't stop between the sounds. Get ready. Move under each sound. Hold. *Mmmaaa.*
Return to the first ball of the arrow. Again. Get ready. Move under each sound. Hold. *Mmmaaa.*
Good saying **mmmaaa.**

e. Call on different children to do *b* or *d.*

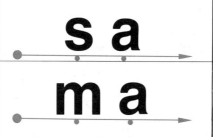

Lesson 4

Sound-Out Teaching Techniques

- Practice presenting step *a* to your partner. In step *a*, you say **sssaaa**. Do not pause between the sounds when you move from ball to ball.
- Present step *b* to your partner, who will not make any mistakes. Reinforce the sounding out at step *b* by saying, "Good saying **sssaaa**."
- Practice steps *c* and *d*. Reinforce at step *d* by saying, "Good saying **mmmaaa**."

Corrections

If the children stop between the sounds at step *b* or *d* or say the incorrect sounds, stop them immediately. Tell the children what they did, and then repeat step *a* (model) and return to step *b* (test), or repeat *c* and return to *d*.

Prereading Take-Home Activities (Lessons 1–16)

The prereading activities you have been practicing involve only the teacher-presentation material. Other prereading activities are included as part of the daily take-home activities presented at the end of each lesson.

Take-Home Signal

Because many take-home tasks require the children to look at symbols on their take-home, you use audible signals to direct the children. The simplest signals are claps. The timing for these signals is exactly the same as it is for the other signals you have practiced.

Sound-Out Teaching Techniques (Sounds)

Part of a take-home is reproduced below. Note that each sound (**s** and **ē**) is on a ball and arrow. At step *a*, the children put their fingers on the first ball of the first arrow. The children have learned the wording *first* and *next* in the sequencing games.

Practice task 4 with your partner. Be sure that your partner is touching the correct starting ball. If not, move your partner's finger and repeat the step.

TASK 12 Children move their finger under s or ē and say it

a. Everybody, finger on the first ball of the first arrow. Check children's responses. When I clap, quickly move your finger under the sound and say it. (Pause.) Get ready. Clap. Children move their finger under **s** and say **sss**.
Yes, **sss**.

b. Again. Finger on the first ball of the first arrow. Check children's responses. Get ready. Clap. Children move their finger under **s** and say **sss**.
Yes, **sss**.

c. Repeat *b* until firm.

d. Everybody, finger on the first ball of the next arrow. Check children's responses. When I clap, quickly move your finger under the sound and say it. (Pause.) Get ready. Clap. Children move their finger under **ē** and say **ēēē**.
Yes, **ēēē**.

e. Again. Finger on the first ball of the arrow. Check children's responses. Get ready. Clap. Children move their finger under **ē** and say **ēēē**.
Yes, **ēēē**.

f. Repeat *e* until firm.

TASK 13 Individual test

a. Call on a child. Show the child which ball to touch. Get ready. Clap. *Child moves finger under the sound and says it.*

b. Call on different children to do *a*.

c. Good. You really know how to move your finger under the sound and say it.

Lesson 4

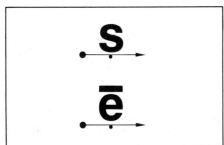

Take-Home 4

The timing of the clap signal is very important. If the timing is questionable, the children will glance up at you. They will be able to respond together and on signal if the time between "Get ready" and the clap is always the same, always predictable. If you have trouble maintaining a precise time interval, try tapping your foot, as if in time with a march. Time your "Get ready . . . Clap" so that it is in time with the tapping, or use a metronome, or practice in time with a recording of a march.

Sound-Out Teaching Techniques (Words)

For this activity, you say the sounds and the children move under them.

TASK 14 Children touch under the sounds

a. Hold up side 1 of your take-home. Touch the first ball of the arrow for **am**. Put your finger on the first ball of this arrow. Check. Put down your take-home.

b. I'm going to say the sounds without stopping. You're going to touch under the sounds as I say them. Quickly move your finger under each sound when I say it. I'll say the sounds you touch. Get ready. **aaammm**. Hold each sound for two seconds. Check that the children are moving their finger under each sound as you say it.

c. Again. Finger on the first ball of the arrow. Check children's responses. Get ready. **Aaammm**. Hold each sound for two seconds. Check that the children are moving their finger under each sound as you say it.

d. Repeat *c* until firm.

Lesson 4

Take-Home 4

Sound-Out Teaching Techniques

The most important teaching technique is the timing of the task. Use the same timing for "Get ready . . . aaammm" as you used for the preceding format ("Get ready . . . Clap").

Corrections

If a child does not move under the appropriate sound as soon as you start to say it, guide the child's finger as you repeat step *c* of the format. After the child can perform with no prompting (such as your guiding the child's finger), repeat step *c* at least two or three more times, until the child's response is firm.

If the children have trouble when you call on them for individual turns, repeat step *c* with the group.

READING

Lessons 1 to 9 set the stage for word reading. Starting at lesson 10, the children begin to read simple, regular words by sounding out each word and saying it fast. Sounds and words are introduced on a closely integrated schedule:

1. By lesson 10, the children have learned six sounds. The children begin to read words containing those sounds. As each new sound is taught, the sound is introduced in words.

2. After a word has been taught and practiced, the word is incorporated in stories or sentences. Once a word has been introduced, it is used throughout the remainder of the program.

3. The children begin to read very short, single-sentence stories in lesson 21.

4. The children practice words and sentences in the independent work on their take-homes.

Comprehension activities are specified in word-reading, story-reading, and take-home activities. Story-reading activities start with basic, literal-comprehension questions. As the children become more proficient, they work on comprehension activities that require judgments or predictions about story events.

How to Use This Section of the Guide

The Reading section of this guide consists of two primary tracks: Reading Vocabulary and Story Reading. Starting at lesson 17, you present both tracks every day. Before you reach lesson 10, you should begin studying and practicing the reading tasks. You may want to do this in three phases:

Phase I: Before your top group reaches lesson 10
Reading Vocabulary. Read the overview (pages 22-23) and practice the formats for regular words (pages 23-25) and rhyming words (pages 26-27).
Story Reading. Read the overview (pages 32-33) and practice the formats for sound it out and say it fast (pages 34-37).

Phase II: When your top group reaches lesson 22
Reading Vocabulary. Practice the formats for reading the fast way (pages 28-30).
Story Reading. Practice the formats for reading the fast way (pages 38-44).

Phase III: When your top group reaches lesson 39
Reading Vocabulary. Practice the formats for irregular words (pages 30-31) and read the information on other reading-vocabulary formats (pages 31-32).
Story Reading. Review the materials on individual checkouts (pages 44-45) and practice the format for read the items (page 46).

READING VOCABULARY
(Lessons 10–80)

Overview

1. The first word-reading (reading vocabulary) formats are introduced in lesson 10. In lessons 13 to 16, the children read words on their take-homes. Beginning at lesson 17, the children read stories composed of words that have been introduced earlier.

2. The first reading-vocabulary words begin with continuous sounds like **a, m, s,** or **th.** Some words may *end* with a stop sound like **d, t,** or **c,** but none *begin* with a stop sound. Sounding out a word that begins with a stop sound is much more difficult than sounding out a word that begins with a continuous sound. Words beginning with stop sounds are introduced at lesson 19, after the children have been reading simple, regular words for nine lessons.

3. In lesson 18, the first "slightly irregular" word is taught. The word is **is.** It is irregular because it is sounded out as **iiisss** (which rhymes with **miss**) but is pronounced **iz.** The teacher directs the children to sound out the word **is** and then "translates" by saying, "Yes, **iz.** We say **iz.** She **is** happy."

Other slightly irregular words presented in early lessons are **a** and **has.** Slightly irregular words are introduced to make the children aware that not everything they read is perfectly regular. By introducing some words that are not perfectly regular early in the reading program, you alert the children to what will come. Note that the children still sound out all words—regular or irregular—but they learn to discriminate between how the irregular word is sounded out and how it is pronounced.

4. Highly irregular words are introduced after the children have mastered slightly irregular words. The procedure is the same—the children always say the sound they have learned for each letter. In sounding out a word such as **was**, they say *wwwaaasss* (rhymes with **mass**). Then you translate, "That's how we **sound out** the word. Here's how we **say** the word. **Wuz**." After several lessons, the children read the whole word the fast way and *then* sound it out. The sounding-out decoding skill eliminates guessing. Irregulars are not treated as "sight" words because a particular word, like **was**, is always spelled the same way. The sounding out demonstrates this stable spelling.

5. The children begin to read words the fast way in lesson 27. By lesson 47, the children read all words the fast way.

A variety of word-attack skills is taught. The same word may appear in a rhyming, a sound-out, a read-the-fast-way, and a build-up format.

The reading-vocabulary portion of the lesson should take no more than ten minutes early in the program and less later in the program, so that an increasing amount of the lesson time can be spent on the stories. The exercises in this guide will help you teach economically.

Although the emphasis of the reading-vocabulary activities is on decoding, we want to make sure the children understand that they are reading real words. Therefore, the program specifies "meaning" sentences to be presented after the children read certain words. For instance, after they read the word **an** in lesson 21, you are instructed to say, "A dog is (pause) **an** (pause) animal." Meaning sentences are not specified for all words. If you feel that a sentence would help the children understand a particular word that may not be well understood in isolation, put it in a sentence. But *don't* use the meaning sentence as a substitute for decoding. Children do not become facile at decoding words by understanding the words. They become facile at decoding by practicing decoding.

Regular Words (Lessons 10–80)

Regular words, such as in the sentence **Pam had a ham**, are easy to read. Each word can be sounded out and said fast without mispronouncing the word. But the number of simple, regular words is very limited. To increase the number of "regular" words (words that children can pronounce the way they are sounded out), Fast Cycle I uses a modified orthography, or print, which is faded out in Fast Cycle II.

Children Say the Sounds, Then Sound Out the Word   (Lessons 10–12)

The first reading-vocabulary format requires a simple extension of the behaviors that have been taught in the say-it-fast—rhyming, and the sound-out formats. Note that the word the children read is presented on an arrow, with a ball beneath each sound. After lesson 23 the arrow is retained, but the balls are removed.

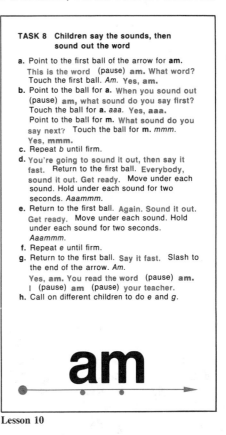

TASK 8   Children say the sounds, then sound out the word

a. Point to the first ball of the arrow for **am**. This is the word (pause) **am**. What word? Touch the first ball. *Am*. Yes, **am**.

b. Point to the ball for **a**. When you sound out (pause) **am**, what sound do you say first? Touch the ball for **a**. *aaa*. Yes, **aaa**. Point to the ball for **m**. What sound do you say next? Touch the ball for **m**. *mmm*. Yes, **mmm**.

c. Repeat *b* until firm.

d. You're going to sound it out, then say it fast. Return to the first ball. Everybody, sound it out. Get ready.   Move under each sound. Hold under each sound for two seconds. *Aaammm*.

e. Return to the first ball. Again. Sound it out. Get ready.   Move under each sound. Hold under each sound for two seconds. *Aaammm*.

f. Repeat *e* until firm.

g. Return to the first ball. Say it fast.   Slash to the end of the arrow. *Am*. Yes, **am**. You read the word (pause) **am**. I (pause) **am** (pause) your teacher.

h. Call on different children to do *e* and *g*.

am

Lesson 10

Point-and-Touch Signal

In steps *b* and *c*, you point to the ball for a sound. Then you touch the ball. The children respond when you touch. Be sure you lift your finger when you move along the arrow so you can point to the next sound without touching it.

Practice pointing and touching in steps *b* and *c*. When you point, be careful not to hide part of the sound from the children's view. Point from below and use the same timing that you use for all other signals.

TASK 8 Children say the sounds, then
        sound out the word

a. Point to the first ball of the arrow for **am**.
   This is the word (pause) **am**. What word?
   Touch the first ball. *Am.* Yes, **am**.

b. Point to the ball for **a**. When you sound out
   (pause) **am**, what sound do you say first?
   Touch the ball for **a**. *aaa.* Yes, *aaa*.
   Point to the ball for **m**. What sound do you
   say next? Touch the ball for **m**. *mmm*.
   Yes, *mmm*.

c. Repeat *b* until firm.

d. You're going to sound it out, then say it
   fast. Return to the first ball. Everybody,
   sound it out. Get ready. Move under each
   sound. Hold under each sound for two
   seconds. *Aaammm.*

e. Return to the first ball. Again. Sound it out.
   Get ready. Move under each sound. Hold
   under each sound for two seconds.
   Aaammm.

f. Repeat *e* until firm.

g. Return to the first ball. Say it fast. Slash to
   the end of the arrow. *Am.*
   Yes, **am**. You read the word (pause) **am**.
   I (pause) **am** (pause) your teacher.

h. Call on different children to do *e* and *g*.

am

Lesson 10

Sound-It-Out—Say-It-Fast Signal

The signal you use to direct the children to sound out
words in steps *d* through *g* of this format (and in all
sound-out formats until lesson 113) is exactly the same
as you practiced for the Sound Out track. (See page
20.) After the children sound out the word, you direct
them to say it fast.

The illustration below demonstrates the correct
procedure for presenting the word **meat**. Practice this
procedure.

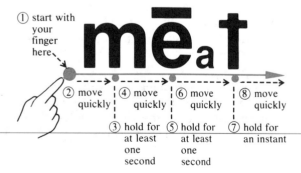

① start with your finger here

② move quickly
③ hold for at least one second
④ move quickly
⑤ hold for at least one second
⑥ move quickly
⑦ hold for an instant
⑧ move quickly

⑨ return to the first ball

⑩ quickly move along arrow for say-it-fast signal

• Hold under the **m** for at least one second; hold
  under the **e** for at least one second; move past the **a**
  (it has no ball under it); hold under the **t** *for only
  an instant*; and then move quickly to the end of the
  arrow. The children respond, *mmmeeet*.

• After you reach the end of the arrow, return to the
  first ball of the arrow. Say, "Say it fast." Pause
  one second. Then slash from the first ball to the
  end of the arrow. The children respond, *meat*.
  Remember, first you talk—then you signal. Practice this timing. Start with your finger on the first
  ball. Keep your finger on the ball as you say, "Say
  it fast...." and pause one second. Signal by slashing
  along the arrow.

Practice task 8 from the beginning, with your partner
making no mistakes.

Corrections

• If the children don't respond firmly for each sound,
  say, "Starting over...." and repeat step *b* until the
  children reliably say both sounds. Present a
  delayed test by repeating steps *a* and *b*.

• Use the correction below for steps *d* through *h* if a
  child breaks between the sounds (*aaa...mmm*) or is
  unable to say the word fast after sounding it out
  (*aaammm*). Your correction will show the children
  how word reading relates to the oral-blending tasks
  they have already learned.

1. Teacher: Everybody, say (pause) *aaammm*. Get
   ready. Hold up a finger for each sound.
2. Group: *aaammm*.
3. Teacher: Say it fast. Drop your hand.
4. Group: *am*.
5. Teacher: Quickly touch the first ball for **am**. Now
   do it here. Sound it out. Get ready. Move quickly
   under each sound. Hold under each sound for two
   seconds.
6. Group: *aaammm*.
7. Teacher: Return to the first ball. Say it fast. Slash
   to the end of the arrow.
8. Group: *am*.
9. Teacher: You did it.

If the mistake occurred on an individual turn, after
correcting the group with steps 1 to 8 above, present
steps *e* and *g* to the child who made the mistake.

Children Sound Out the Word and Say It Fast (Lessons 17–24)

During these lessons, the children read a group of words on a page. A performance criterion is specified. The group must read all the words on the page in order without making a mistake before you present the next page. The children will make some mistakes. When they make a mistake on a word, you correct the mistake and go to the next word. When you finish the last word, you tell the children, "That was pretty good. Let's read the words again. See if you can read them without making a mistake." Return to the first word on the page and present all the words in order until the children meet the page criterion.

READING VOCABULARY
Do not touch any small letters.
As soon as you read all the words on this page without making a mistake, we'll go on to the next page.

TASK 7 Children sound out the word and say it fast

a. Touch the first ball of the arrow for **sēēd**. Sound it out. Get ready. Move quickly under each sound. *Sssēēēd.*
b. Return to the first ball. Again, sound it out. Get ready. Move quickly under each sound. *Sssēēēd.*
c. Repeat *b* until firm.
d. Return to the first ball. Say it fast. Slash. *Seed.*
   Yes, what word? *Seed.*
   Plant a (pause) **seed.**

sēēd

TASK 8 Children sound out the word and say it fast

a. Touch the first ball of the arrow for **is**. Sound it out. Get ready. Move quickly under each sound. *Iiisss.* (Children should not say **iiizzz**.)
b. Return to the first ball. Again, sound it out. Get ready. Move quickly under each sound. *Iiisss.*
c. Repeat *b* until firm.
d. Return to the first ball. Say it fast. Slash. *Is.* Yes, **iz**. We say, **iz**. She (pause) **is** (pause) working hard today.

is

TASK 9 Children sound out the word and say it fast

a. Touch the first ball of the arrow for **rēad**. Sound it out. Get ready. Move quickly under each sound. *Rrrēēd.*
b. Return to the first ball. Again, sound it out. Get ready. Move quickly under each sound. *Rrrēēd.*
c. Repeat *b* until firm.
d. Return to the first ball. Say it fast. Slash. *Read.* Yes, what word? *Read.*

TASK 10 Children sound out the word and say it fast

a. Touch the first ball of the arrow for **mē**. Sound it out. Get ready. Move quickly under each sound. *Mmmēē.*
b. Return to the first ball. Again, sound it out. Get ready. Move quickly under each sound. *Mmmēē.*
c. Repeat *b* until firm.
d. Return to the first ball. Say it fast. Slash. *Me.*
   Yes, what word? *Me.*

CRITERION

If the children read the words in tasks 7, 8, 9, and 10 without making any mistakes, present individual turns.
If the children made mistakes, say: That was pretty good. Let's read the words again. See if you can read them without making a mistake.

TASK 11 Individual test

Call on different children. Each child is to do task 7, 8, 9, or 10.

Lesson 20

Note: The word **is** is slightly irregular. It is sounded out as **iiisss**, but it is pronounced **iz**, not **iss**. This word was introduced in lesson 18. In lessons 18 through 20, the children sound the word out and say it fast, *iss*, after which you say, "Yes, **iz**. We say **iz**." At lesson 21, the children continue to sound out the word as *iiisss*, but they are familiar enough with the word to pronounce it correctly when you tell them to say it fast.

Rhyming Words (Lessons 15–80)

Beginning at lesson 15, the children read some words as rhyming words by applying the rhyming skills they practiced in the oral rhyming tracks.

The rhyming skill allows the children to read many new words by blending different initial sounds with word endings. A child with good rhyming skills can see that words that rhyme have ending parts that sound alike and look alike.

In each rhyming format in lessons 15 to 25, a series of two or more words is presented. The rhyming part of each word is in red type. The beginning sounds are in black type. Children sound out and identify the ending part. Then they identify the beginning sound and blend it with the ending part.

Rhyming—Words That Begin with Continuous Sounds

- *Steps b to d.* Use the same signal as you practiced in the sound-it-out—say-it-fast formats on page 24.
- *Step e.* Keep your finger on the first ball of the arrow for **mad** as you ask, "So what does this word rhyme with?" Tap the ball. The children respond, *ad.* Keep touching the first ball until after you say, "Rhyme with (pause) **ad**. Get ready...." Move quickly to the second ball and hold. The children respond, *mmm.* When you slash, they complete the unblended word—*mmmad*. Return to the first ball. Keep touching the ball as you ask, "What word?" Pause one second. Slash. The children should say, *mad.*

Corrections—Step e

1. When you tap the first ball of the arrow, the children may respond by saying *mmm*, because they are not attending to your question. If they say *mmm*, correct by saying *ad.* **It rhymes with *ad*. Listen again.** Repeat step e from the beginning.
2. When you hold your finger under the **m**, the children are supposed to hold the **mmm** until you slash. If a child says *mmad* before you slash, tell the group, **I'm still touching under the *mmm*.** Repeat step e from "Rhyme with (pause) **ad**. Get ready," until the children are firm at holding the **mmm**.

TASK 14   Children rhyme with ad

a. Point to **ad, mad,** and **sad.** These words rhyme.
b. Touch the first ball of the arrow for **ad** (Pause.) Sound it out. Get ready. Move quickly under each sound. *Aaad.*
c. Return to the first ball. Again, sound it out. Get ready. Move quickly under each sound. *Aaad.*
d. Return to the first ball. Say it fast. Slash. *Ad.* Yes, **ad.**
e. Touch the first ball of the arrow for **mad.** The red part of this word is (pause) **ad.** So what does this word rhyme with? Tap the ball. *Ad.* Yes, **ad.** Rhyme with (pause) **ad.** Get ready. Move quickly to the second ball. Hold. *mmm.* Slash. *Mmmad.* Return to the first ball. What word? Slash. *Mad.* Yes, **mad.**
f. Touch the first ball of the arrow for **sad.** The red part of this word is (pause) **ad.** So what does this word rhyme with? Tap the ball. *Ad.* Yes, **ad.** Rhyme with (pause) **ad.** Get ready. Move quickly to the second ball. Hold. *sss.* Slash. *Sssad.* Return to the first ball. What word? Slash. *Sad.* Yes, **sad.**
g. Call on different children to do e or f.

Lesson 17

Rhyming—Words That Begin with Stop Sounds

Words that begin with stop sounds, such as **c, d,** or **t,** are hard for children to sound out because the sound cannot be held for more than an instant. If the sound is held longer, it becomes distorted with an inappropriate vowel sound—**duuuuuu.** A variation of the word-rhyming format teaches children to process words that begin with stop sounds (lessons 19 to 25).

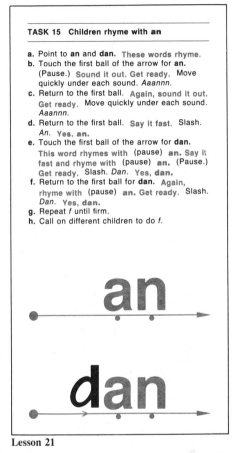

TASK 15   Children rhyme with an

a. Point to **an** and **dan.** These words rhyme.
b. Touch the first ball of the arrow for **an.** (Pause.) Sound it out. Get ready. Move quickly under each sound. *Aaannn.*
c. Return to the first ball. Again, sound it out. Get ready. Move quickly under each sound. *Aaannn.*
d. Return to the first ball. Say it fast. Slash. *An.* Yes, **an.**
e. Touch the first ball of the arrow for **dan.** This word rhymes with (pause) **an.** Say it fast and rhyme with (pause) **an.** (Pause.) Get ready. Slash. *Dan.* Yes, **dan.**
f. Return to the first ball for **dan.** Again, rhyme with (pause) **an.** Get ready. Slash. *Dan.* Yes, **dan.**
g. Repeat *f* until firm.
h. Call on different children to do *f.*

Lesson 21

The arrowhead prompts children to say the sound fast and to blend the sound with the ending part of the word. If the stop sound appears at the end of a word, it has a ball under it rather than an arrowhead because the children stop at the end of a word.

Children Read a Word Beginning with a Stop Sound

This format, which starts at lesson 29, contains fewer prompts than earlier rhyming formats. The children first identify the ending part of the word (which is no longer in red), and then they rhyme. Note that there are no balls or arrowheads on the arrow shaft.

TASK 17   Children read a word beginning with a stop sound (hit)

a. Run your finger under **it.** You're going to sound out this part. Get ready. Touch **i, t** as the children say *iiit.*
b. Say it fast. (Signal.) *It.* Yes, this part says (pause) **it.**
c. Repeat *a* and *b* until firm.
d. Touch the ball for **hit.** This word rhymes with (pause) **it.** Get ready. Move quickly along the arrow. *Hit.*
e. What word? (Signal.) *Hit.* Yes, **hit.**
f. Repeat *d* and *e* until firm.
g. Return to the ball. Now you're going to sound out (pause) **hit.** Get ready. Quickly touch **h, i, t** as the children say *hiiit.*
h. What word? (Signal.) *Hit.* Yes, **hit.** Good reading. She **hit** me.
i. Repeat *g* and *h* until firm.

Lesson 29

- *Step a.* Run your finger under **it** to identify the part of the word the children are to sound out. Do not permit them to start sounding out with **h.** If necessary, cover the **h.**
- *Step b.* You say, "Say it fast," and not, "What word?" because the ending part of a stop-sound word is not always a word by itself (**tail, cop, he**).
- *Step d.* Quickly touch the **h** for only an instant, and then slash under the rest of the word as the children say, *hit.*
- *Step g.* Touch the **h** for only an instant, and then move to **i.** The illustration below shows your behavior for directing the sounding out of this word, which begins (and ends) with a stop sound.

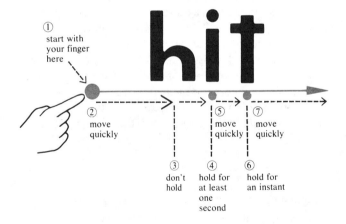

Correction

If children have trouble with step *g,* remind them, **You have to say this first sound fast. So I can't stop under it. When I stop under the next sound, say both sounds.**

Reading the Fast Way (Lessons 27–47)

The sequence of formats in this track is designed to help the children make the transition from sounding out every word to reading new words without sounding them out. Beginning at lesson 27, the children read a word the fast way after they have sounded out the word and identified it.

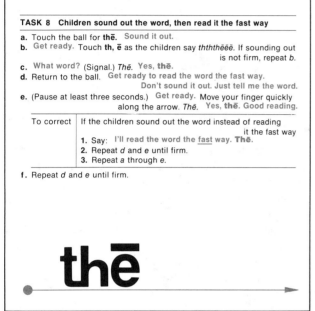

Lesson 27

- *Steps b and c.* Touch under each sound as the children sound out the word. Slash under the word as the children respond to "What word?"
- *Step e.* Pause at least three seconds. The idea is to build the child's "memory" for handling words. If you proceed too fast from *c* through *e*, very little memory load will be placed on the child. In later formats, the memory load will be further increased until the children are able to remember words consistently from one day to the next.
- *Steps d and e.* Expect to repeat these steps at least one time the first time this format is presented.

Correction

If a child misidentifies the word at step *e*, correct by returning to step *a* and repeating the task.

Track Development

In the first format for **in** shown below, you count to five before directing the children to identify the word. The purpose of the counting is to challenge the children to remember the word in the face of greater "interference."

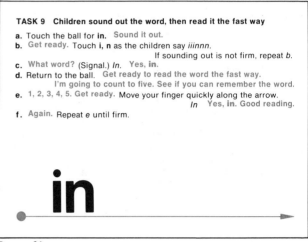

Lesson 31

Some words are in shaded boxes. The children have read these words earlier in the lesson.

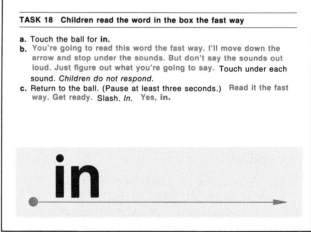

Lesson 31

Word-identification mistakes are corrected by first directing the children to sound out the word and then repeating the task.

A reading-vocabulary page from lesson 36 is reproduced below. Tasks 15 and 16 are rhyming tasks.

TASK 15   Children rhyme with sick

a. Touch the ball for **sick.** Sound it out.
b. Get ready. Touch **s, i, c** as the children say *sssiiic.*
   If sounding out is not firm, repeat *b.*
c. What word? (Signal.) *Sick.* Yes, **sick.**
d. Quickly touch the ball for **lick.** This word rhymes with (pause)
   sick. Get ready. Touch **l.** *lll.* Move your finger quickly along the
   arrow. *Lllick.*
e. What word? (Signal.) *Lick.* Yes, **lick.**

TASK 16   Children read a word beginning with a stop sound (hāte)

a. Run your finger under **āte.** You're going to sound out this part.
   Get ready. Touch **ā, t** as the children say *āāāt.*
b. Say it fast. (Signal.) *Ate.* Yes, this part says (pause) **ate.**
c. Repeat *a* and *b* until firm.
d. Touch the ball for **hāte.** This word rhymes with (pause) **āt.**
   Get ready. Move quickly along the arrow. *Hate.*
e. What word? (Signal.) *Hate.* Yes, **hate.**
f. Repeat *d* and *e* until firm.
g. Return to the ball. Now you're going to sound out (pause) **hate.**
   Get ready. Quickly touch **h, ā, t** as the children say *hāāāt.*
h. What word? (Signal.) *Hate.* Yes, **hate.** Good reading. Do you **hate**
   monsters?
i. Repeat *g* and *h* until firm.

TASK 17   Individual test

Call on different children to do *g* and *h* in task 16.

TASK 18   Children read the words the fast way

a. Now you get to read these words the fast way.
b. Touch the ball for **lick.** (Pause three seconds.) Get ready.
   Move your finger quickly along the arrow. *Lick.*
c. Repeat *b* for the words **sick** and **hāte.**
d. Have the children sound out the words they had difficulty identifying.

TASK 19   Individual test

Call on different children to read one word the fast way.

Do not touch any small letters.

siCk

liCk

hāTe

Lesson 36

Children Read the Fast Way

Beginning at lesson 47, the children read all the words on the page the fast way and then read the words in a new, random order as specified in the format. Beginning at lesson 47, most words will be taught in this format.

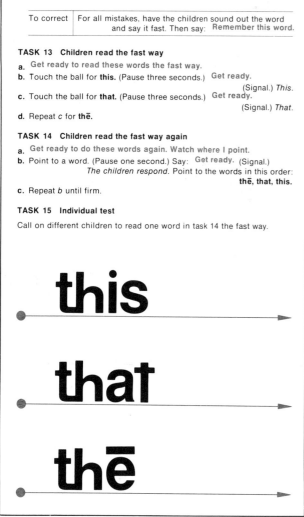

To correct	For all mistakes, have the children sound out the word and say it fast. Then say: Remember this word.

TASK 13   Children read the fast way

a. Get ready to read these words the fast way.
b. Touch the ball for **this**. (Pause three seconds.) Get ready. (Signal.) *This.*
c. Touch the ball for **that**. (Pause three seconds.) Get ready. (Signal.) *That.*
d. Repeat *c* for **thē**.

TASK 14   Children read the fast way again

a. Get ready to do these words again. Watch where I point.
b. Point to a word. (Pause one second.) Say: Get ready. (Signal.) *The children respond.* Point to the words in this order: **thē, that, this.**
c. Repeat *b* until firm.

TASK 15   Individual test

Call on different children to read one word in task 14 the fast way.

this
that
thē

Lesson 47

- Treat the page as a unit. The children must be able to read all the words on the page correctly before moving to the next page.
- Follow the specified variation in order when the children reread the words. Varying the original order will show you just how firm the children really are on all the words.
- In the rereading, pause one second after pointing to a word before signaling for the children to say the word. If you signal without pausing, they will probably have difficulty responding correctly.

Irregular Words (Lessons 43–80)

Before lesson 43, you introduced slightly irregular words, such as **has, is, a**. Now you will introduce somewhat more irregular words, such as **was, saw, said, boy**. In Reading Mastery, a word is irregular if it is sounded out one way and pronounced (said fast) another.

An irregular word is introduced in stages through several lessons. In the first stage, the word is sounded out and then pronounced as it is usually said. In the next stage, the word is identified by reading it the fast way, and then sounding it out. The word then appears on reading-vocabulary pages to be read the fast way.

Children Sound Out an Irregular Word (First Format)

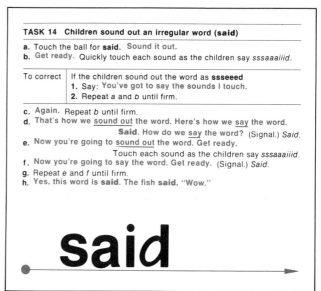

TASK 14   Children sound out an irregular word (said)

a. Touch the ball for **said**. Sound it out.
b. Get ready. Quickly touch each sound as the children say *sssaaaiiid*.

To correct	If the children sound out the word as **ssseeed**
	1. Say: You've got to say the sounds I touch.
	2. Repeat *a* and *b* until firm.

c. Again. Repeat *b* until firm.
d. That's how we <u>sound out</u> the word. Here's how we <u>say</u> the word. **Said**. How do we <u>say</u> the word? (Signal.) *Said.*
e. Now you're going to <u>sound out</u> the word. Get ready. Touch each sound as the children say *sssaaaiiid*.
f. Now you're going to say the word. Get ready. (Signal.) *Said.*
g. Repeat *e* and *f* until firm.
h. Yes, this word is **said**. The fish **said**, "Wow."

said

Lesson 43

- *Step d.* Emphasize the words *sound out* and *say*. Pause slightly to set off the words. "That's how we (pause) **sound out** the word. Here's how we (pause) **say** the word. **Said.** How do we (pause) **say** the word?" Signal by slashing along the arrow.
- *Steps e and f.* Repeat these steps in sequence at least two times. With very low-performing children, you may have to present the sequence four or five times before the children are firm. Expect these children to have difficulty with the first two or three irregular words that are introduced.

Corrections

1. In step *e*, if the children sound out the word the way it is pronounced, say the correct sound (ăăă), and then use the correction in the format.

2. In step *f*, if the children begin to sound out the word when told to say the word or if they say the wrong word, correct as follows:

step f ⟶ Now you're going to say the word. Get ready. (Signal.)

mistake ⟶ Children say *sssaaaiiid* or *was*. Correct by saying, That word is *said*. Say the word. Get ready. (Signal.) *Said (sed)*. Now sound out the word. Get ready. (Signal.) *Sssaaaiiid*. Let's try it again. Return to step *a*.

Children Sound Out an Irregular Word (Second Format)

After three lessons, the irregular word is taught with this format.

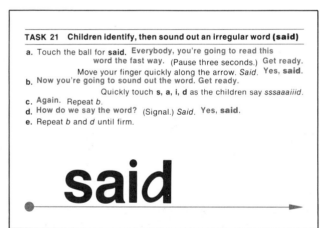

TASK 21 Children identify, then sound out an irregular word (said)

a. Touch the ball for **said.** Everybody, you're going to read this word the fast way. (Pause three seconds.) Get ready. Move your finger quickly along the arrow. *Said.* Yes, **said.**
b. Now you're going to sound out the word. Get ready. Quickly touch **s, a, i, d** as the children say *sssaaaiiid.*
c. Again. Repeat b.
d. How do we say the word? (Signal.) *Said.* Yes, **said.**
e. Repeat b and d until firm.

Lesson 45

- *Step a.* Be sure to pause three seconds to give the children thinking time.

Corrections

Use the same corrections as for the first irregular-word format.

Special Word-Analysis Formats

Beginning with lesson 47, the children read vocabulary words the fast way, except in the following special word-analysis formats.

Ending Build-Ups (Lessons 66–80)

The children read the first word, *kiss.* You touch the ball for **kiss** and say, "Yes, this word is **kiss.**" You quickly touch the ball for **kissed** and say, "So this must be kiiiiissssssss...." and point to the **d** before touching it. When you touch the **d,** the children say, *kissed.* Then they sound out the word. You signal for the sounding-out as you would if the word were on an arrow like the one below.

Move quickly from the **k** to the **i,** then to between the two **s**'s, and then to the **d.**

In teaching this particular build-up, avoid avoid referring to the ending as "the e–d ending." Such a reference might lead the children to mispronounce the ending. In some of the words the children read, the ending is pronounced **d** as in **rained**; in others it's pronounced **t** as in **kissed.** If the children pronounce **kissed** with a **d** sound, say, "Yes, **kisst.** What word?"

**Words Beginning with Two Consonants
(Lessons 65—80)**

You cover the **s**; the children identify the last part of the word—*lip*. You uncover the **s** and tell the children, "First you say **sss**; then you say **lip**." The children blend *ssslip*, and then say it fast. After they are firm, the children sound out the word.

STORY READING (Lessons 17—80)

The content of the stories is based on two main criteria: First, the words used in the stories are coordinated carefully with the words introduced in the reading-vocabulary presentations. Words are generally presented in the reading-vocabulary presentation for a few days before they are introduced in the stories. Second, the stories and art are designed to be interesting, amusing, and appealing to the children.

All story-reading exercises are part of the structured lesson. They follow the sounds and reading-vocabulary exercises. The allotted lesson time permits the group to read each story more than one time. Initially, the stories are not the major part of the reading lesson. By lesson 36, however, most of the lesson time is spent on story reading. The stories range in length from 2 words in lesson 17 to more than 150 words by lesson 80.

Overview

The major topics in the Story track are outlined in the scope and sequence chart on page 100. In this Story Reading section of the guide, each topic is described and teaching techniques and corrections are provided.

Sounding Out Words (Lessons 10—35)

During this lesson range, children sound out each word and then say it fast. Sounding out begins in reading vocabulary at lesson 10. The children sound out one word on their take-homes in lessons 13 to 16. In lessons 17 to 20, they sound out two words on their take-homes. Three- and four-word stories start on take-home 21.

You model how to read the fast way after the children sound out the story words in lessons 17 to 23. In lessons 24 to 35, the children learn the skills they need to make the transition from sounding out to reading the fast way.

Reading Words the Fast Way (Lessons 36—80)

The children identify whole words when they read the fast way. Whole-word reading begins in reading vocabulary at lesson 27. In story 36, the children read sentences the fast way. By lesson 47 in reading vocabulary, the children read most words the fast way. In stories 54 through 80, the children no longer sound out words; but sounding out continues to be used in the correction procedure.

Individual checkouts begin at lesson 54. For a checkout, each child reads part of the story the fast way. You time the reading. A rate and accuracy criterion is specified.

Comprehension (Lessons 10—80)

Comprehension of reading-vocabulary words begins in lesson 10 with the introduction of "meaning" sentences. Starting at lesson 17, comprehension skills are taught within the Story track through the oral questions you present, through discussion of the pictures for the stories, and through written questions on the take-homes.

Pictures. In lessons 17 to 51, the story and the picture related to the story are not on the same page. Children use the words they read to predict something about the contents of the picture. Then they look at the picture as you ask questions. At this point in the program, the emphasis is on making sure the children comprehend what they read. They first read the words; *then* they look at the picture. They do not use "picture cues" to help them figure out words because pictures do not imply specific words.

Oral Questions. From lessons 36 to 80, you ask comprehension questions during the reading of the story. The questions and the points at which they are to be asked are specified. Many questions deal with *who, what, where, when, why,* and *how.* For another type of question, you summarize story events and ask the children to predict what will happen next. For questions that can be answered directly from the words in the story, you signal for a group response. For questions that call for diverse responses—such as, "What do you think?"—you call on individual children.

Written Questions. In lessons 66 to 80, the children answer written questions about the story. These questions are on the take-homes.

Read the Items. In lessons 76 to 80, the children play a game called Read the Items. The items are not intuitively obvious, and therefore call for careful teaching and understanding. For example, the children read, "If the teacher says 'go,' stand up." To play the game, the children must remember the instructions because you will say different things, such as "stand up" and "go." (Children are to respond only to "go" for this item.)

Additional Skills (Lessons 21–69)

Through a series of exercises in lessons 21 through 69, the children learn a set of skills that facilitate their whole-word reading and sentence reading. These exercises include practice in word finding, sentence saying, period finding, quotation finding, question-mark finding, reading the title, word practice, and review of troublesome words.

Student Materials for Story Reading

The children's stories for lessons 17 through 43 are in Take-Home Books A and B. The stories for lessons 44 through 80 are in Storybook 1. Stories for Fast Cycle II (lessons 81 through 170) are in Storybook 2.

Some take-homes between lessons 49 and 80 have an extra page on which one of the children's stories is duplicated. You tell the children," I'll give you a bonus take-home. That is an extra take-home for doing a good job." The children color the picture and take the story home.

Two-part stories begin at lesson 73. The second part of a story begins with a summary of what happened during the first part.

How to Conduct Group Story Activities

1. Seat the children so that they are all close to you and can see the presentation book. Sit so that you can observe whether each child's finger is pointing to the words and whether each child's mouth is forming the words.

2. Seat the higher-performing children on the ends of the group. Place the lower-performing children in the middle of the group.

3. Give all children lap boards or large books on which to place their take-home or storybook.

4. Do not allow the children to turn the page to look at the picture until you tell them to turn the page.

5. Each time you give an instruction to point, quickly check that each child is pointing appropriately.

6. During reading, make sure that the children look at the words, not at you.

7. Use an audible signal to elicit responses.

8. Make sure that you listen most frequently to the lowest-performing children in the group.

Sounding Out Words (Lessons 10–35)

Children Sound Out the Word and Say It Fast

During lessons 17 to 20, the children do not read actual stories; they read two isolated words on their take-home sheets. The illustration below presents the words **me** and **eat**. The children sound out each word and then say the word fast. Then individual children read one of the words. You model reading the words the fast way. The children use one of the words as a basis for predicting what they will see in a picture on the other side of the take-home. The children look at the picture and answer some questions that relate to it.

TASK 14 Children sound out the first word and say it fast

a. Pass out Take-Home 20. Do not let the children look at the picture until task 18.

b. Hold up side 1 of your take-home. Point to **mē** and **ēat**. You're going to read these words.

c. Everybody, touch the first ball for the first word. Check children's responses. Look at the sounds in the word and figure out what you're going to say. (Pause three seconds.)

d. Sound it out. Get ready. Clap for each sound, pausing about two seconds between claps. Children move their finger under each sound as they say *mmmēēē*.

e. Again, finger on the first ball. Check children's responses. Sound it out. Get ready. Clap for each sound, pausing about two seconds between claps. *Mmmēēē*.

f. Repeat *e* until firm.

g. Everybody, say it fast. (Signal.) *Me.* What word? (Signal.) *Me.* Yes, **me.**

h. Repeat *e* and *g* until firm.

TASK 15 Children sound out the next word and say it fast

a. Everybody, touch the first ball for the next word. Check children's responses. After you read that word, you'll see a picture for that word. Look at the sounds in the word and figure out what you're going to say. (Pause three seconds.)

b. Sound it out. Get ready. Clap for each sound, pausing about two seconds between claps. Children move their finger under each sound as they say *ēēēt*.

c. Again, finger on the first ball. Check children's responses. Sound it out. Get ready. Clap for each sound, pausing about two seconds between claps. *Ēēēt*.

d. Repeat *c* until firm.

e. Everybody, say it fast. (Signal.) *Eat.* What word? (Signal.) *Eat.* Yes, **eat.**

f. Repeat *c* and *e* until firm.

TASK 16 Individual test

a. Everybody, follow along with your finger as I call on different children to read one of the words.

b. Everybody, touch the first ball for the first word. Check children's responses. Call on a child. Sound it out. Get ready. Clap for each sound, pausing about two seconds between claps. *Mmmēēē.* Say it fast. (Signal.) *Me.* Yes, **me.**

c. Everybody, touch the first ball for the next word. Check children's responses. Call on a child. Sound it out. Get ready. Clap for each sound, pausing about two seconds between claps. *Ēēēt.* Say it fast. (Signal.) *Eat.* Yes, **eat.**

d. Call on different children to do *b* or *c*.

TASK 17 Teacher reads the fast way

a. Hold up your take-home.

b. Touch the first ball of the arrow for **ēat.** Everybody, I'm going to read this word the fast way. Slash as you say: **eat.** I read it the fast way.

c. Touch the first ball of the arrow for **ēat.** I'll read it again. Slash as you say: **eat.**

TASK 18 Picture comprehension

a. You've read the word (pause) **eat.** Now you're going to see a picture. The boy in the picture has a sack with something to . . . . (Signal.) *Eat.* Yes, **eat.** The boy in the picture has a sack with something to . . . . (Signal.) *Eat.*

b. Everybody, turn your take-home over and look at the picture. Check responses.

c. Ask these questions:
1. Show me the sack. *The children respond.*
2. Can you see something to (pause) **eat** in that sack? *The children respond.* He might have apples or popcorn.
3. Why is the boy dressed up that way? *The children respond.* Yes, for Halloween.
4. Did you ever dress up for Halloween? *The children respond.*
5. What did you wear? *The children respond.*

Lesson 20

Take-Home 20, Side 1

Take-Home 20, Side 2

Task 14 Teaching Techniques

- *Step a.* Do not let the children look at the picture until task 18. You want them to read the word before they relate it to the picture. Enforce this rule.

- *Step c.* Be sure that the children figure out the sounds in the word **mē** before sounding it out. If the children are not obviously attending to the sounds, tell them to move under each sound and say it to themselves. Pause at least three seconds before beginning the sounding out. This pause is critical to give the children time to look at the sounds.

- *Step d.* Pause about two seconds between claps. Check to see that the children are touching under each sound as you clap. (They practiced this behavior on take-homes 4 to 12.) The children are not to stop between the sounds when they say them.

- *Step e.* Be sure that the children are touching the first ball for **mē**.
- *Step g.* Give an audible signal—a clap or a snap—for the children to say the word fast. They must be looking at their papers, not at you.

Tasks 16–18 Teaching Techniques

- *Task 16.* Check to see that all the children are following along with their fingers as different children read one of the words. You may have to move some children's fingers.
- *Task 17.* Be sure that the children are looking at your take-home as you model how to read the word the fast way.
- *Task 18, step a.* Be sure the children are looking at you.
- *Task 18, step c.* The children should be looking at the picture. Do not signal. Let different children respond. But do not let the discussion continue for more than about ten seconds.

Corrections

Correct sound misidentification by telling (modeling) the correct sound and repeating the step in which the mistake occurred.

Correct touching errors by physically moving the children's fingers and repeating the step. If the children stop between the sounds, present a model by calling on an individual to sound out the word.

If the children cannot say a word fast, correct as you did in reading vocabulary (page 24) by changing the task into an oral task. Then direct the children to sound out and identify the word on their take-home.

Remember to follow each correction with a repetition of the step that was missed.

Following is a series of correction procedures for word-identification errors on group reading or on individual tests. If you compare the procedures, you'll see that they are similar to each other, with only slight variations. For group reading, the last step in the correction in lessons 17 to 20 involves repeating the *word* that was missed. In lessons 21 to 80, it involves repeating the *sentence* that was missed.

Similarly, for an individual test, in lessons 17 to 45, the last step in the correction involves repeating the *word* that was missed, while in lessons 46 to 80, the last step involves repeating the *sentence* that was missed.

Learn these correction procedures and refer back to them as you work through the story formats in this guide.

Group Reading, Lessons 17–20
Correction for Word-Identification Errors

The correction involves the following steps:

1. Identifying the word
2. Directing the group to sound out and identify the word
3. Repeating the steps for sounding out the word

The group is reading the word **mē** (lesson 20, task 14, steps *e, f,* and *g.*) Jim and Ed make mistakes at step 4.

1. <u>Teacher</u>: Again, finger on the first ball. Check children's responses. Sound it out. Get ready. Clap for each sound, pausing about two seconds between claps.
2. <u>Group</u>: *Mmmēē.*
3. <u>Teacher</u>: Everybody, say it fast. (Signal.)
4. <u>Jim</u>: *Eēē.*
   <u>Terry</u>: *Mē.*
   <u>Ed</u>: *Mēēt.*
5. <u>Teacher</u>: That word is *mē.* Everybody, finger on the ball. Check. Sound it out. Get ready. Clap for each sound, pausing about two seconds between claps.
6. <u>Group</u>: *Mmmēēē.*
7. <u>Teacher</u>: Everybody, say it fast. (Signal.)
8. <u>Group</u>: *Mē.*
9. <u>Teacher</u>: What word? (Signal.)
10. <u>Group</u>: *Mē.*
11. <u>Teacher</u>: Yes, *mē.* Good. You said it fast. Starting over. Return to step *e* and present steps *e, f,* and *g.*

Individual Test, Lessons 17–45
Correction for Word-Identification Errors

The correction involves the following steps:

1. Identifying the word
2. Directing the group to sound out and identify the word
3. After giving other children individual tests, requiring the child who made the mistake to sound out the word and identify it

Individual test on the word **ēat** (lesson 20, task 16, step *c*). Lola makes a mistake at step 4.

1. Teacher: **Everybody, touch the first ball for the next word.** Check children's responses. **Lola, sound it out. Get ready.** Clap for each sound, pausing about two seconds between claps.
2. Lola: *Eēēt*.
3. Teacher: **Say it fast.** (Signal.)
4. Lola: *At*.
5. Teacher: **That word is** *ēat*. **Everybody, finger on the ball.** Check. **Sound it out. Get ready.** Clap for each sound, pausing about two seconds between claps.
6. Group: *Eēēt*.
7. Teacher: **Everybody, say it fast.** (Signal.)
8. Group: *Eat*.
9. Teacher: **Yes,** *ēat*. Continue with task 16. After completing task 16, return to Lola.
10. Teacher: Point to the ball for **ēat**. **Lola, touch the ball for this word.** Check. **Sound it out. Get ready.** Clap for each sound, pausing about two seconds between claps.
11. Lola: *Eēēt*.
12. Teacher: **Say it fast.** (Signal.)
13. Lola: *Eat*.
14. Teacher: **Yes,** *ēat*. **Good. You said it fast.**

Group Reading, Lessons 21–80
Correction for Word-Identification Errors

Take-Home 21

The correction involves returning to the beginning of the sentence and rereading the sentence.

1. Identify the word. **That word is....**
2. Direct the group to sound out and identify the word. **Everybody, sound it out. Get ready.... What word?**
3. Direct the group to return to the first word of the sentence and read the entire sentence. **Starting over,** or **Back to the first word (of the sentence).**

Until the words **period** and **sentence** have been taught, you will show the children where to start rereading.

Individual Test, Lessons 46–80
Correction for Word-Identification Errors

a littlₑ fish sat on a fat fish.

Story 46

The correction involves returning to the beginning of the sentence and rereading the sentence:

1. Identify the word. **That word is....**
2. Direct the group to sound out and identify the word. **Everybody, sound it out. Get ready.... What word?**
3. Require the child who made the mistake to sound out the word and identify it. **Sound it out. Get ready.... What word?**
4. Direct the child to return to the first word of the sentence and read the entire sentence. **Back to the first word of the sentence.**

Sounding-Out-Words Track Development

Boxes Between the Words (Lessons 21–42)

Three- and four-word stories begin in lesson 21. Boxes on the line between the words keep the children from running the words together. You establish the terminology of "first word" and "next word" by directing the children to touch the beginning ball for the *first word* and to sound the word out. Then they touch the box for the *next word* and sound it out.

Take-Home 22

Starting at lesson 25, there are no balls under the sounds in the words, but you continue to clap for each sound and the children continue to touch under the sounds. At lesson 26, the boxes move above the line. They gradually get smaller, until they are phased out at lesson 43.

Teacher and Children Read the Fast Way
(Lessons 24–35)

In lessons 17 to 23, you modeled how to read the fast way after the children sounded out the words in the story. In lessons 24 to 35, you and the children read part of the story the fast way. You provide a strong model of inflection and whole-word reading. The lower-performing children, especially, need this strong model; so be sure to teach these exercises to criterion.

TASK 17 Teacher and children read the fast way

a. Point to the words on the first arrow. Touch under **it.**
    Everybody, this word is (pause) **it.** What word? (Signal.)
                        It. Yes, **it.** Remember that.
b. We're going to read this story the fast way.
c. Point to **sit on.** I'll read these words the fast way.
d. Point to **it.** When I touch this word, you're going to say . . . .
                                  (Signal.) *It.* Yes, **it.**
e. Repeat *d* until firm.
f. Touch the ball of the arrow. Reading the fast way. (Pause three
                seconds.) Touch under **sit on** and say: Sit on . . . .
g. Then touch under **it.** *It.*
h. Repeat *f* and *g* until firm.
i. Yes, **sit on it.**

Lesson 26

---

sit ▪ on ▪ it.

Take-Home 26

- *Step a.* After you ask, "What word?" move to the end of the arrow. The children should respond, *it.*
- *Step d.* Signal the children to complete the sentence. Watch your voice cue and your timing. Say, "When I touch this word, you're going to saaaaaay...." and move to the end of the arrow.
- *Step f.* After you say, "Reading the fast way," be sure to pause for three seconds. Move quickly to **sit** and say, "**sit.**" (If you move slowly, the children may try to respond with you.) Then move quickly to **on** and say, "**on.**"
- *Step g.* Move more slowly to **it.** Children are to respond the instant you stop under the word, not before.
- Repeat steps *f* and *g* until the children are firm. Then say, "Yes, **sit on it.**"

Correction

Use this correction procedure for step *g* if the children begin to sound out the word instead of saying it fast.

1. (*Model*) Immediately say the word, it.
2. (*Lead*) Repeat steps *f* and *g*, responding with the children at step *g.* Repeat the lead.
3. (*Test*) Repeat step *f.* Then present step *g.* Do not respond with the children.

4. (*Delayed Test*) Say, Let's do it again. Return to step *a* and present the format. Do not lead the children at step *g.*

Dotted Arrows Between the Lines (Lessons 28–35)

Beginning with lesson 28, the stories are printed on two lines.

this ▪ is
not ▪ mē.

Take-Home 28

The dotted arrow from the first line to the second line is a prompt for the children. Some children have a tendency to go from the end of the first line to the end of the second line. The dotted arrow prompts children to begin the next line at the left. The dotted arrow is dropped at lesson 36, after the children have mastered the convention of proceeding from line to line.

TASK 17 Children follow the arrow to the bottom line

a. Pass out Take-Home 28. Do not let the children look at the picture
                                until task 22.
b. Point to the story. These words are on two lines. Watch me touch
                                all the words.
c. Touch **this** and **is.** Now I follow the arrow to the ball on the next
                                line. Follow the arrow.
d. Now I touch the rest of the words. Touch **not** and **me.**
e. Repeat *b* through *d* two times.
f. Your turn. Finger on the ball of the top line.
                          Check children's responses.
g. Touch the words when I clap. Get ready. Clap for **this** and **is.**
                          (The children respond.)
h. Now follow the arrow to the next ball. Check children's responses.
i. Repeat *f* through *h* until firm.
j. Touch the words on the bottom line when I clap. Get ready.
                Clap for **not** and **me.** *(The children respond.)*
k. This time you're going to touch all the words in the story.
        Finger on the ball of the top line. Check children's responses.
                        Get ready. Clap for **this** and **is.**
l. Do not clap for **not** until the children have followed the arrow to the
                ball on the bottom line. Then clap for **not** and **me.**
m. Repeat *k* and *l* until firm.

Lesson 28

- *Step f.* Be sure to refer to the first line as the *top* line and stress the word **top.** You are using the word **first** in connection with **first word** and **first sound.**
- *Step l.* If the children do not move their fingers to the ball of the second line, you may have to tell them, "Go to the next ball," or, "Follow the arrow to the next ball." Remember to present the delayed test after any corrections. Repeat steps *k* and *l* until firm.

Reading the Fast Way (Lessons 36—80)

Throughout the word-reading activities in the Reading Vocabulary and Story tracks, the emphasis is on increasing the children's ability to decode without sounding out words. The steps that lead to whole-word reading are sequenced so that the children are able to relate the attack skill of sounding out words to the skill of remembering words. Children do not lose the ability to sound out words; they simply add the ability to remember words. This combination gives them the tools they need to figure out new words and the strategy they need to note the details of words and remember them.

Do not clap for any small letters.

TASK 20 First reading—children sound out each word and tell what word

a. Pass out Take-Home 36. Do not let the children look at the picture until task 22.
b. Get ready to read the story. First word. Check children's responses.
c. Get ready. Clap for each sound. *Hēēē.* What word? (Signal.) *He.* Yes, **he.**
d. Next word. Check children's responses.
e. Get ready. Clap for each sound. *Aāāt.* What word? (Signal.) *Ate.* Yes, **ate.**
f. Repeat *d* and *e* for the remaining words in the story.

TASK 21 Second reading—children reread the story and answer questions

a. This time you'll read the story and I'll ask questions. Back to the first word. Check children's responses.
b. Repeat *c* through *f* in task 20. Ask the comprehension questions below as the children read.

After the children read:	You say:
He ate a fig.	What did he eat? (Signal.) *A fig.*
And he is sick.	How does he feel? (Signal.) *Sick.* Why? (Signal.) *Because he ate a fig.*
To correct	If the children do not give acceptable answers, have them reread the sentence that answers the question. Then ask the question again.

TASK 22 Picture comprehension

a. What do you think you are going to see in the picture? *The children respond.*
b. Turn your take-home over and look at the picture.
c. Ask these questions:
   1. Is he eating a fig? *The children respond.* No.
   2. Why is he sick? *The children respond.* He ate a fig.
   3. What is that thing in his mouth? *The children respond.* A thermometer.
   4. What's the doctor going to do to make him feel better? *The children respond.*

TASK 23 Word finding

a. Turn your take-home back to side 1. Everybody, look at the words in the top line. One of the words is **he.**
b. Get ready to touch **he** when I clap. (Pause three seconds.) Get ready. Clap. *(The children touch hē.)*
c. Repeat *b* for these words: **fig, hē, āte, fig, āte, fig, hē, āte, hē, fig, āte.**

TASK 24 Children read the first sentence the fast way

a. Everybody, now you're going to read part of the story the fast way. Finger on the ball of the top line. Check children's responses.
b. Move your finger under the sounds of the first word and figure out the sounds you're going to say. Don't say the sounds out loud. Just figure out what you're going to say. Check children's responses. Prompt children who don't touch under the sounds. (Pause five seconds.) Read the word the fast way. Get ready. Clap. Say *he* with the children. *He.*
c. Next word. Move your finger under the sounds and figure out the sounds. Check children's responses. (Pause five seconds.) Read the word the fast way. Get ready. Clap. Say *ate* with the children. *Ate.*
d. Repeat *c* for the words **a, fig.**
e. Let's read the words the fast way again. Everybody, finger on the ball of the top line. Check children's responses. Figure out the first word and get ready to read it the fast way. Say the sounds to yourself. (Pause five seconds.) What word? Clap. *He.* Yes, **he.**
f. Figure out the next word. Say the sounds to yourself. (Pause five seconds.) What word? Clap. *Ate.* Yes, **ate.**
g. Repeat *f* for the words **a, fig.**

TASK 25 Individual test

a. Everybody, finger on the ball of the top line. Check children's responses.
b. We're going to have different children read. Everybody's going to touch the words.
c. Everybody, touch the first word. Check children's responses.
d. Call on a child. Reading the fast way. Get ready. Clap. *He.*
e. Next word. Check children's responses.
f. Everybody reading. Get ready. Clap. *Ate.*
g. Next word. Check children's responses.
h. Call on a child. Get ready. Clap. *A.*
i. Repeat *e* and *f* for **fig.**

Lesson 36

hē ▪ āt$_e$ ▪ a ▪ fig.
anᵈ ▪ hē
is ▪ sic$_k$.

Take-Home 36, Side 1

Take-Home 36, Side 2

Reading the Fast Way, Lesson 36

Starting with lesson 36, a number of changes appear in the procedures for reading the take-home story.

- On the first reading, the children use familiar procedures to sound out each word one time and tell what word.
- On the second reading of the story, you ask questions at specified points in the reading.
- After the second reading, the children look at the picture, and you ask questions about it.
- Next, the children play word finding with three words that appear in the top line of the story.
- Then, the children read the first sentence the fast way—a new activity.
- Finally, for the individual test, you mix group reading and individual reading.

Task 20. Sounding Out Words That Begin with Stop Sounds

The children sound out each word only one time before they identify the word. In earlier lessons, you clapped for each sound, pausing two seconds between claps as the children held each sound. But the word **hē** begins with a stop sound, and there is no way the children can hold a stop sound. If you pause two seconds between claps, the children must either pause between the stop sound and the next sound or mispronounce the stop sound. To guide the sounding out, you must clap for **h** and then quickly for **ēēē**. Children should not stop between the sounds as they say . . .

Children: hēēē

Note that the children say both sounds in response to your second clap. For the word **him**, you would clap for **h**; clap quickly for **iii** as the children say **hiii**; and clap quickly for **mmm**.

Task 23. Word Finding

Word-finding activities started at lesson 26 as a transition activity between sounding out words and reading words the fast way. In lesson 36, task 23, an abbreviated form of the activity is presented.

- *Step a.* Make sure the children are looking at the words and not at you or at their neighbor's story.
- *Step b.* Make sure the children are pointing to the appropriate word before you signal.
- *Step c.* Repeat the series until the children are firm.

Correction

If a child touches a wrong word, have the child sound out and identify that word. **Sound out the word you're touching. Get ready.... What word? Is that the word** *fig*? **Look for the word** *fig, fffiiig.*

Task 24. Children Read the First Sentence the Fast Way

This is a new kind of reading task. The children reread the first sentence the fast way. *You clap one time for each word.*

- *Step b.* If the children don't move their fingers under the sounds, guide their fingers. Pause five seconds before saying, "Read the word the fast way." Count to yourself or tap your foot five times. You must pause long enough before saying "Get ready" to allow the children to figure out the word. Some children will audibly sound out the word as they point to the sounds. This behavior is quite acceptable. If the children sound out too loudly, tell them to whisper. But allow them to go through the familiar steps of sounding the word out. Say "Get ready," clap, and say "**he**" with the children.
- *Steps c and d.* Repeat the procedures for the remaining words in the first sentence.
- *Step e.* Note that you ask, "What word?" and clap, but you *do not lead* by saying the word with the children. You reinforce by saying, "Yes, **he**."
- *Steps f and g.* Repeat the procedures for the remaining words in the first sentence.

Correction

Use the same correction procedure you used for word-identification errors. (See page 36.)

Reading-the-Fast-Way Track Development

- In lessons 36 to 42, the children read the first sentence the fast way.
- In lesson 43, the children are taught to find the periods and to say a sentence.
- In lesson 43, the children read the first two sentences the fast way.
- In lesson 44, the children reread the entire story the fast way.
- In lessons 54 to 80, the children read the story the fast way on the first reading.

TASK 21 Period finding

a. Turn your take-home back to side 1. Everybody, we're going to read all the words in the first sentence the fast way.

b. Point to the first word. The first <u>sentence</u> begins here and goes all the way to a little dot called a period. So I just go along the arrow until I find a period.

c. Touch **a.** Have I come to a period yet? (Signal.) *No.*
   Touch **fish.** Have I come to a period yet? (Signal.) *No.*
   Touch **māde.** Have I come to a period yet? (Signal.) *No.*
   Touch **a.** Have I come to a period yet? (Signal.) *No.*
   Touch **wish.** Have I come to a period yet? (Signal.) *Yes.*

d. Again. Repeat *b* and *c* until firm.

e. Everybody, put your finger on the ball of the top line.
   Check children's responses.

f. Get ready to find the period for the first sentence. Go along the arrow until you find that period. Check children's responses.

TASK 22 Children read the first sentence the fast way

a. Everybody, get ready to read all the words in the first sentence the fast way.

b. Touch the first word. Check children's responses.
   (Pause three seconds.) Get ready. Clap. *A.*

c. Next word. Check children's responses. (Pause three seconds.)
   Get ready. Clap. *Fish.*

d. Repeat *c* for the words **made, a, wish.**

e. After the children read **wish,** say: Stop. That's the end of the sentence.

f. Let's read that sentence again, the fast way.

g. First word. Check children's responses. Get ready. Clap. *A.*

h. Next word. Check children's responses. Get ready. Clap. *Fish.*

i. Repeat *h* for the words **made, a, wish.**

j. After the children read **wish,** say: Stop. You've read the first sentence.

TASK 23 Children read the second sentence the fast way

a. Everybody, put your finger on the period after **wish.**
   Check children's responses.

b. Now move along the arrows until you find the next period.
   Check children's responses.

c. Repeat *a* and *b* until firm.

d. Put your finger on the period after **wish.**
   Check children's responses.

e. Get ready to read all the words until we come to the next period.

f. Starting with the first word after **wish.** Check children's responses.
   (Pause three seconds.) Get ready. Clap. *I.*

g. Next word. Check children's responses. (Pause three seconds.)
   Get ready. Clap. *Wish.*

h. Repeat *g* for the remaining words in the second sentence.

i. After the children read **feet,** say: Stop. You've read the sentence.

j. Let's read it again. Go back to the period after **wish.**
   Check children's responses.
   Get ready to read all the words in the sentence.

k. First word. Check children's responses. Get ready. Clap. *I.*

l. Next word. Check children's responses. Get ready. Clap. *Wish.*

m. Repeat *l* for the remaining words in the second sentence.

TASK 24 Individual test

a. Everybody, finger on the ball of the top line.
   Check children's responses.

b. We're going to have different children read the fast way.
   Everybody's going to touch the words.

c. First word. Check children's responses. Call on a child. Clap.
   The child responds.

d. Next word. Check children's responses. Call on a child.
   Clap. *The child responds.*

e. Repeat *d* for the remaining words in the first sentence.

TASK 25 Sentence saying

Good reading. Now, everybody, say all the words in that sentence without looking. (Signal.) *The children repeat the sentence at a normal speaking rate.*

.a fish māde a wish.
."I wish I had feet. I wish
.I had a tāil. I wish I had
.a hat. I wish I had a dish."

Take-Home 43

Task 21. Period Finding

In task 21, you introduce the words **period** and **first sentence.** In tasks 22 and 23, you tell the children when they have come to the end of a sentence. When they are firm on these tasks, the children will understand the relationship between a period and a sentence.

Task 22. Children Read the First Sentence the Fast Way

- *Step b.* Practice the timing. Say, "Touch the first word." Scan the children's pointing fingers. Watch their mouths forming the words. Pause three seconds. Say, "Get ready." Clap.

- *Steps c and d.* As soon as the children respond, say, "Next word" . . . Scan . . . Pause three seconds . . . Say, "Get ready" . . . Clap.

- *Steps g and h.* Continue to use the three-second pause, although it is not specified.

Task 23. Children Read the Second Sentence the Fast Way

Maintain your three-second pause in steps *f* through *h* before you clap for each word. Reduce the length of the pause in steps *j* through *m.*

- *Step j.* A signal is not specified for finding a period because all children cannot be expected to find the period at the same time. Some children will move along the line faster than others. In the first few presentations, you may have to tell the children, "Go ahead. Do it."

Task 25. Sentence Saying

This task requires children to remember the words in a sentence. They should say the sentence at a normal, brisk pace with an inflection that conveys the meaning of the sentence. The group should repeat the sentence until all words are properly sequenced and the inflection is appropriate.

If a child omits a word, says the words out of sequence, or inflects inappropriately, repeat the sentence. Then have the children repeat the sentence.

Additional Sentence–Reading Activities

At lesson 46 you introduce quotations; the children answer questions on the first and second reading of the story; and individual children read whole sentences the fast way.

Quotation Finding

> **TASK 24   Quotation finding**
>
> a. Pass out Storybook 1.
> b. Open your book to page 5.
> c. Point to the quotation marks around the word **wow** in the second sentence. These marks show that somebody is saying something. He's saying the word between these marks.
> d. Point to the quotation marks around **that fat fish is mom** in the last sentence. These marks show that somebody is saying something. He's saying all the words between these marks.
> e. Point to the quotation marks around **wow**. Everybody, touch these marks in your story. Check children's responses. Somebody is saying the word between those marks.
> f. Point to the quotation marks around **that fat fish is mom**. Everybody, touch these marks in your story. Check children's responses. Somebody is saying all the words between those marks.
> g. Repeat e and f until firm.

Lesson 46

> a little fish sat on a fat fish.
> the little fish said, "wow."
> the little fish did not hate the
> fat fish. the little fish said,
> "that fat fish is mom."

Story 46

In the first two stories, quotations are in red type. The sentence-saying practice has prepared the children for repeating what is said within quotation marks.

- *Steps c and d.* Be sure to show the children the quotation marks and the word or words between the marks. You can point with two fingers to the set of quotation marks, or you may want to prop the book so you can point to the marks with both hands. When you refer to the words "between the marks," run a finger under the words to which you refer.

- *Steps e and f.* Do not signal. Watch to make sure that the children touch the marks. You may have to help them by placing their index fingers on the quotation marks.

Answering Questions

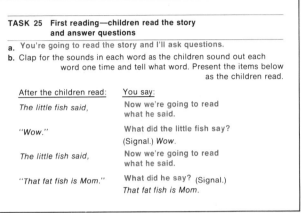

> **TASK 25   First reading—children read the story and answer questions**
>
> a. You're going to read the story and I'll ask questions.
> b. Clap for the sounds in each word as the children sound out each word one time and tell what word. Present the items below as the children read.
>
> | After the children read: | You say: |
> | --- | --- |
> | *The little fish said,* | Now we're going to read what he said. |
> | *"Wow."* | What did the little fish say? (Signal.) *Wow.* |
> | *The little fish said,* | Now we're going to read what he said. |
> | *"That fat fish is Mom."* | What did he say? (Signal.) *That fat fish is Mom.* |

Lesson 46

If the children do not respond on signal at a normal speaking rate, correct by presenting a model, and then a test, as you did for sentence saying. (See page 40.) Then present a delayed test by asking the question again.

Individual Children Read a Sentence the Fast Way

> **TASK 28   Individual test**
>
> a. I'm going to call on different children to read a whole sentence the fast way. Everybody's going to touch the words.
> b. First word of the story. Check children's responses. Call on a child to read the first sentence. Do not clap for each word.
> c. Call on a child to read the second sentence. Do not clap for each word.

Lesson 46

- Individual children read at their own rates; you do not clap. Other children point to the words being read.
- Praise children who read rapidly and accurately. Praise children who read with inflection. Praise children who are trying hard and doing well.
- Provide several individual tests. Be sure to call on some lower-performing children.

Question Mark Finding

TASK 18 First reading—question mark finding

Have the children reread any sentences containing words that give them trouble. Keep a list of these words.

a. Pass out Storybook 1.
b. Open your book to page 9 and get ready to read.
c. Clap for the sounds in each word of the first sentence as the children sound out each word one time and tell what word.
d. After the children read **she was not mad at him**, say: Everybody, move along the lines until you come to the next period. Oh, oh. There's no period in this sentence. There's a funny mark called a question mark.
e. Everybody, touch the question mark. Check children's responses.
f. There's a question mark in this sentence because this sentence asks a question. Everybody, get ready to read the question.
g. Finger on the first word. Check children's responses. Clap for the sounds in each word of the sentence as the children sound out each word one time and tell what word.
h. After the children read **did she hit him?** say: Everybody, say that question. *The children repeat the question at a normal speaking rate.*
i. Yes, **did she hit him?** Let's read the next sentence and find out.
j. Finger on the first word. Check children's responses. Clap for the sounds in each word of the sentence as the children sound out each word one time and tell what word.
k. Did she hit him? (Signal.) *No.*
l. Everybody, get ready to read the next sentence. Repeat g through k for the sentences: **did she hug him? no, no, no.**
m. Everybody, get ready to read the next sentence. Repeat g and h for the last sentence: **did she kiss him?**
n. Did she kiss him? We'll find out later.
o. After the first reading of the story, print on the board the words that the children missed more than one time. Have the children sound out each word one time and tell what word.
p. After the group's responses are firm, call on individual children to read the words.

Lesson 48

.she̅ was not mad at him. did
.she̅ hit him? no̅, no̅, no̅. did she̅
.hug him? no̅, no̅, no̅. did she̅
.kiss him?

Story 48

This format teaches the difference between the question mark and the period. The children read each question in the story, say the question at a normal speaking rate, and read the answer.

Children Read the Fast Way Without Sounding Out (Lessons 54-80)

Major changes take place during these lessons. The children no longer sound out during story reading except as a correction. During group story reading, the group reads the fast way. Individual children read sentences. You present individual checkouts and time each child reading the whole story or part of the story without sounding out.

Procedures for Lessons 54—59

TASK 20 First reading—children read the story the fast way

Have the children reread any sentences containing words that give them trouble. Keep a list of these words.

a. Pass out Storybook 1.
b. Open your book to page 22 and get ready to read.
c. We're going to read the story the fast way.
d. Touch the first word. Check children's responses.
e. Reading the fast way. First word. (Pause three seconds.) Get ready. Clap. *The.*
f. Next word. Check children's responses. (Pause three seconds.) Get ready. Clap. *Old.*
g. Repeat f for the remaining words in the first sentence. Pause at least three seconds between claps. The children are to identify each word without sounding it out.
h. Repeat d through g for the next two sentences. Have the children reread the first three sentences until firm.
i. The children are to read the remainder of the story the fast way, stopping at the end of each sentence.
j. After the first reading of the story, print on the board the words that the children missed more than one time. Have the children sound out each word one time and tell what word.
k. After the group's responses are firm, call on individual children to read the words.

Lesson 54

---

the̅ o̅ld go̅ₐt had an o̅ld co̅ₐt.
the̅ o̅ld go̅ₐt said, "I will e̅ₐt this
o̅ld co̅ₐt." so̅ she̅ did.
"that was fun," she̅ said. "I a̅te
the̅ o̅ld co̅ₐt. and now I am co̅ld."
now the̅ o̅ld go̅ₐt is sad.

Story 54

- Keep a list of troublesome words for word practice at steps *j* and *k*.

- *Steps b through g.* These procedures are similar to those you used for reading the fast way in lessons 43 through 53. (See page 40.)

- *Step h.* You direct the reading and rereading of the first three sentences until the children are firm. Pause at least three seconds before signaling for each word. If the children are firm at reading one word every three seconds, they will be likely to maintain their rate through the rest of the story.

Note that the children reread any sentences that are not firm. Some children will have difficulty reading the fast way at this specified rate. You can pause longer than three seconds before words that you know might take longer to figure out, such as new words, words beginning with a stop sound, or words the children had trouble with during the reading-vocabulary exercises.

The simplest way to determine an appropriate rate for group reading is to direct individual children to read the passage. Note the amount of time each child requires for different words. Based on their performance, adjust the thinking time so that the signal is appropriate for about eighty percent of the children's individual performances. If some children are consistently very slow (requiring more than five seconds per word), provide additional firming before proceeding in the program.

• *Step i.* Children are to stop at the end of each sentence. On the second reading, you will ask questions at the end of some sentences.

Procedures for Lessons 60−80

Beginning with story 57, the stories have titles. In the first story task for lessons 57 through 59, you hold up your storybook, point to the title, and say, "These words are called the **title** of the story. These words tell what the story is about."

TASK 19   First reading—children read the story the fast way

Have the children reread any sentences containing words that give them trouble. Keep a list of these words.

a. Pass out Storybook 1.
b. Open your book to page 38.
c. Everybody, touch the title of the story and get ready to read
the words in the title the fast way.
d. First word. Check children's responses. (Pause two seconds.)
Get ready. Clap. A.
e. Clap for each remaining word in the title.
f. After the children have read the title ask: What's this story about?
(Signal.) *A fish in the rain.* Yes, **a fish in the rain.**
g. Everybody, get ready to read this story the fast way.
h. First word. Check children's responses. (Pause two seconds.)
Get ready. Clap. A.
i. Clap for the remaining words in the first sentence. Pause at
least two seconds between claps.
j. Repeat h and i for the next two sentences. Have the children
reread the first three sentences until firm.
k. The children are to read the remainder of the story the fast way.
stopping at the end of each sentence.
l. After the first reading of the story, print on the board the words that
the children missed more than one time. Have the children
sound out each word one time and tell what word.
m. After the group's responses are firm, call on individual children
to read the words.

Lesson 60

---

a fish in the rain

ron met pat in the rain. ron got wet.
pat got wet.
ron said, "this is not fun."
pat said, "this is fun."
ron said, "I have wet feet. so I
will go home. I do not need rain."
pat said, "we can get fish."
so she got a fish and gave it to him.
ron said, "it is fun to get wet if we
get fish."

Story 60

• *Step h.* Some children may touch the first word of the title instead of the first word of the story. Firm the discrimination by telling the children, "You're not touching the first word of the story." Hold up your storybook and touch the first word of the story. "Here's the first word of the story. Everybody, touch it.... Listen: Everybody, touch the first word of the *title*. Get ready.... Listen: Everybody, touch the first word of the *story*. Get ready...."

• *Step i.* Here are some guidelines for clapping:
1. Slow the pace for the first word in every line after the first line. Say, "Next word," as soon as the children read the last word of a line. Then say, "Get ready...." Clap. Make sure that the children are touching under the first word of the line before you clap.
2. Slow the pace before troublesome words.
3. Use the individual tests and individual rate-and-accuracy checkouts to determine whether the children are reading the words in the group reading or are being led. If their rates on individual tests or checkouts are typically slower than the rate you establish for the group reading, your rate is too fast. If they make a number of errors on individual tests, they are probably being led.
4. Make sure that the children point under the words that are being read—both on group and individual turns. Watch the children's mouths as they form the words, and observe whether the children are pointing appropriately.
5. Except for words that are preceded by "Get ready," all words must be presented at a constant rate.

Fast Cycle I   43

Individual Children or the Group Read Sentences on the First Reading (Lessons 70–80)

TASK 21 Individual children or the group read sentences to complete the first reading

a. I'm going to call on different children to read a sentence.
   Everybody, follow along and point to the words. If you hear a mistake, raise your hand.
b. Call on a child. Read the next sentence. Do not clap for the words. Let the child read at his own pace, but be sure he reads the sentence correctly.

| To correct | Have the child sound out the word. Then return to the beginning of the sentence. |

c. Repeat b for most of the remaining sentences in the story. Occasionally have the group read a sentence. When the group is to read, say: **Everybody, read the next sentence.** (Pause two seconds.) **Get ready.** Clap for each word in the sentence. Pause at least two seconds between claps.

Lesson 70

After the group is firm on the title and the first three sentences, you call on individual children to read a sentence. Intersperse some group turns. Children raise their hands if they hear a mistake. Use the corrections on page 36 to correct the group or the individual.

Individual Checkouts for Rate and Accuracy (Lessons 54–80)

Individual checkouts begin after the children have learned to read stories the fast way on the first reading. They continue through Fast Cycle II. Checkouts appear in the lessons indicated on the chart on page 45. They are presented to the children individually.

The checkouts are very important both for the children and for you. For the children, they provide practice in reading a long passage the fast way. The checkouts also demonstrate to the children that they are to use the strategy of reading the fast way and are not to continue sounding out words.

For you, the checkouts provide information about the children's progress. This information is not a duplication of the mastery-test information. The checkouts show you in detail whether the children are progressing acceptably, whether additional firming is needed, whether the children tend to make particular mistakes you hadn't observed, and whether individuals should be placed in a different part of the program.

To pass a checkout, a child must read a selection within a specified period of time and must make no more than a specified number of errors. The length of the selections, the time, and the acceptable number of errors vary from checkout to checkout, but these details are specified in the checkout instructions.

Below is a format from lesson 54. It describes the checkout procedure.

TASK 30 2½-minute individual checkout

Make a permanent chart for recording results of individual checkouts. See Teacher's Guide for sample chart.
a. As you are doing your take-home, I'll call on children one at a time to read the **whole story.** If you can read the whole story the fast way in less than two and a half minutes and if you make no more than three errors, I'll put two stars after your name on the chart for lesson 54.
b. If you make too many errors or don't read the story in less than two and a half minutes, you'll have to practice it and do it again. When you do read it in under two and a half minutes with no more than three errors, you'll get one star. Remember, two stars if you can do it the first time, one star if you do it the second or third time you try.
c. Call on a child. Tell the child: **Read the whole story very carefully the fast way. Go.** Time the child. If the child makes a mistake, quickly tell the child the correct word and permit the child to continue reading. As soon as the child makes more than three errors or exceeds the time limit, tell the child to stop. You'll have to read the story to yourself and try again later. Plan to monitor the child's practice.
d. Record two stars for each child who reads appropriately. Congratulate those children.
e. Give children who do not earn two stars a chance to read the story again before the next lesson is presented. Award one star to each of those children who meet the rate and accuracy criterion.

END OF LESSON 54

Lesson 54

Firming

If more than one-third of the children in the group fail to pass checkouts at lessons 57 and 95, you should carefully examine your teaching procedures because the children are not performing acceptably. Pay particular attention to the way you present all reading-vocabulary tasks, and make sure that you are presenting a sufficient number of individual turns to the lower performers in the group. Also, consider placing the children who do not pass the checkouts on the first trial in a group that is at an earlier lesson in the program.

If the children make more than the maximum number of errors specified and do not complete the checkout selection in the specified time, do not work on reading rate. Work on accuracy, and do not encourage the children to try to read fast. Simply give them a lot more practice at reading accurately. As their accuracy improves, praise them when they read faster, but make it very clear that they are to read accurately.

If the children make errors because they are trying to read fast, tell them to slow down. The rates that are specified for checkouts should be easily attained by the children without rushing. Remember, the first priority is accuracy; rate will follow with practice and reinforcement.

Some teachers prepare children for checkouts by directing the children to read to other children in the class or to practice reading silently before the checkout.

Sometimes you may be unable to complete the checkout during one lesson. If all checkouts are not completed, finish the checkouts on the following day.

Record the results of the individual checkouts on a copy of the Rate and Accuracy Chart, which appears on page 97 of this guide. The chart may be reproduced for your classroom use. A sample chart is shown below. In the column for lesson 54, two stars indicate that David read the story on the first trial in under two and a half minutes with no more than three errors. Joan's star was awarded on the second or third trial. Kristen did not pass the checkout.

You may want to add *Time* and *Number of Errors* to your chart.

Rate and Accuracy Chart

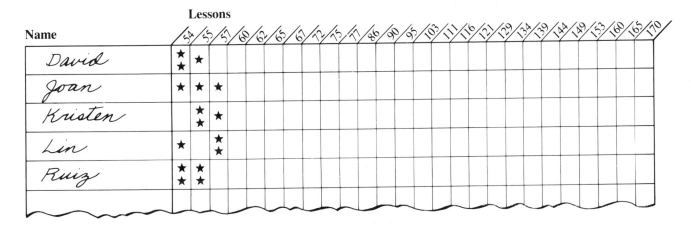

Read the Items (Lessons 76–80)

Read the items is a vehicle for teaching and testing comprehension skills. The items the children read are designed so that the children must read every word and remember the instructions given in the item. The tasks are presented so that you can test the children to make certain that they are reading carefully and comprehending. The first format, at lesson 76, has only one item.

TASK 23   Children read item 1

a. Pass out Storybook 1.
b. Open your book to page 85.
c. Point to the title **rēad the ĭtem**. Everybody, touch this title.
Check children's responses.
d. I'll read the title. You point to the words I read. (Pause.)
Get ready. **Read** (pause) **the** (pause) **item**.
e. Your turn to read the title. First word. Check children's responses.
Get ready. Clap for each word as the children read *read the item*.
f. Everybody, say the title. (Pause and signal.)
Without looking at the words, the children say *read the item*.
Repeat until firm.
g. You're going to read the item. Touch item 1 and get ready to read.
Check children's responses.
h. First word. Clap for each word as the children read:
If the teacher says "Now," hold up your hand.
Repeat three times or until firm.
i. Everybody, get ready to say item 1 with me. (Pause and signal.)
Without looking at the words, you and the children say: If the teacher says "Now," (pause one second) hold up your hand.
Repeat four times or until firm.
j. All by yourselves. Say item 1. (Signal.) *If the teacher says "Now," hold up your hand.* Repeat four times or until firm.

TASK 24   Children reread item 1 and answer questions

a. Everybody, touch item 1 again. Check children's responses.
b. Read item 1 to yourself. Raise your hand when you know what you're going to do and when you're going to do it.
c. After the children raise their hands, say: Everybody, what are you going to do if I say "**Now**"? (Signal.) *Hold up my hand.*

To correct	1. Everybody, read item 1 out loud. Clap as the children read each word.
	2. What are you going to do if I say "**Now**"? (Signal.) *Hold up my hand.*

d. Everybody, when are you going to **hold up your hand**? (Signal.) *If the teacher says "Now."*

To correct	1. Everybody, read item 1 out loud. Clap as the children read each word.
	2. When are you going to **hold up your hand**? (Signal.) *If the teacher says "Now."*

e. Repeat *c* and *d* until firm.

TASK 25   Children play the game

a. Everybody, touch item 1. Check children's responses.
b. Read the item to yourself. Raise your hand when you know what you're going to do and when you're going to do it.
c. After the children raise their hands, say: Let's play the game.
Think about what you're going to do (pause) and when you're going to do it.
d. Hold out your hand. (Pause.) Get ready. **Now**. (Pause.)
Drop your hand. *(The children hold up their hands immediately.)*

To correct	1. What did I say? (Signal.) *Now.*
	2. What are you supposed to do if I say "**Now**"? (Signal.) *Hold up my hand.*
	3. If the children's responses are not firm, have them read item 1 aloud.
	4. Repeat task 25.

Lesson 76

```
          rēad the Item
I. if the tēacher says "now," hōld up your hand.
```
Story 76

- *Task 23, step h*. Pause after the word **now**. This helps the children divide the statement into parts that relate to the two comprehension questions you will ask in task 24.
- *Task 23, steps i and j*. Be sure the children repeat what they have read at a normal speaking rate.
- *Task 24, step b*. Do not insist that the children read silently. They may whisper or read in a low voice.
- *Task 24, steps c and d*. Give the children some thinking time in steps *c* and *d*. Hold the last word that you say in step *c*—**nowwww**.

Correction

The corrections for tasks 24 and 25 are specified in the formats. You correct the children by referring them to the item for the answer to the question.

TAKE-HOMES

Overview

The take-homes support many skills that are taught in the Reading Mastery program and shape the children's ability to work independently. Each take-home presents four or more different activities and will usually occupy the children in independent work for fifteen to thirty minutes. The take-homes for lessons 13 to 43 also contain the words and stories that the children read.

The take-home serves an important function when the children begin to read. It allows children to relate what goes on in school to what goes on at home. It provides parents with a potential basis for praising their child's performance in school. Equally important, it shows parents on a day-to-day basis what is happening in school and what their child is being taught. The take-home extends and reinforces the teacher-directed activities.

When new take-home activities are introduced, they are teacher-directed. After one or two days of such direction, the children work on the activities independently. When the children work independently, they should work with as little help from you as possible. Early in the program, some children may need help with writing. Work with these children and praise them for progress in working independently.

The Work Check

Check the children's take-home work each day. Mark errors in pencil or in some way that your marks can be erased so the parent will see a corrected paper. Set up a simple rule that the children must have everything corrected on their take-homes before they take them home. Pay close attention to the take-homes. The children's performance on their take-homes reflects how well they have learned a particular skill. If you see a pattern of errors, reteach that skill.

Rewarding the Children

Set up a point system for rewarding children who complete their independent work with few errors during the allotted time.

For no errors on the take-home	10 points
For 1 to 3 errors	2 points
For more than 3 errors	0 points

Make a chart that shows the number of points that each child earns each day. At the end of the week, have an awards ceremony at which the children can exchange their points for tangible rewards. These can be inexpensive puzzles or games, class parties, or special certificates of award that the children can take home, stating that "John earned 26 points this week for hard work on his take-homes."

A reasonable number of points to qualify a child for the awards ceremony is 26.

Summary of Independent Activity

After the children have learned how to do a particular kind of exercise, it becomes part of their independent activity. At the end of each lesson, you indicate to the children which take-home exercises they will complete independently. These activities are specified for you in the last tasks for each lesson.

Take-Home Track Development

Each of the take-home activities shown on the scope and sequence chart on page 106 is developed in a sequence of increasing complexity. The exact steps for teaching these activities are detailed in tasks that appear at the end of each lesson in the presentation books.

The take-home formats in the presentation books are self-explanatory, carefully detailed, and easy to follow. You should become familiar with them before teaching the take-home activities. The first time a new format appears in the presentation book, its title has lines above and below it. Follow the directions carefully during the days you present the task to the children. Your careful, exact presentation will pay off in fewer errors when the children begin doing the tasks independently.

The following take-home activities will be discussed in this guide: writing, pair relations, and reading comprehension.

Sound Writing (Lessons 1–80)

The children write sounds every day of Fast Cycle I. They practice the sounds they have already learned.

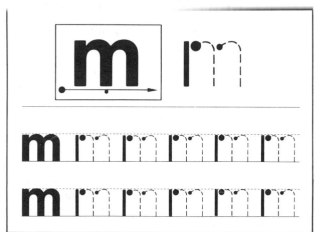

Take-Home 1

At first you will have to provide additional practice for children who have difficulty forming the symbols. Some of your lower performers may need help in handling a pencil or crayon.

Gradually the sound-writing exercises change so that only a part of the symbol is traced and the rest is done freehand. The change begins at lesson 5.

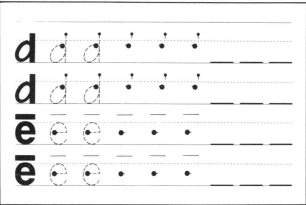

Take-Home 10

By lesson 17, the children will be making several different symbols freehand on the same sheet.

Story Copying and Sentence Copying (Lessons 17–80)

These take-home exercises teach the children to copy an entire story; later, part of a story; and, finally, a sentence that is similar to a sentence in the story. In the first exercise, at lesson 17, the children copy directly below the story. They trace the letters by following the dotted lines on the first arrow. In early lessons, blocks appear between the words and there are macrons over the long vowels. All the letters in the words the children write are full-size. Blocks are printed to show the children where they are to write each word.

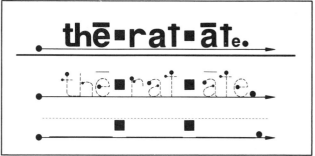

Take-Home 27

Watch the children carefully to be sure they are writing the letters small enough to fit into the available space. Be sure that they complete one word at a time. The children may try copying a whole row of the first letter, then a row of the next letter, and so on. This defeats the purpose of the exercise—to practice writing whole words.

Starting at lesson 44, the children write a sentence related to the story and illustrate the sentence.

The writing exercises reinforce the sounds and words being taught. They are not intended to replace a handwriting program.

Pair Relations (Lessons 5-71)

Children who complete the pair-relations exercises are in a good position to understand the kind of workbook activities they will encounter in a variety of school subjects and on standardized tests. For all pair relations, a symbol must be paired with the appropriate object or an illustration paired with the appropriate sentence. The examples below show some of the various types of pair-relations exercises in the program.

Children complete the pairs.

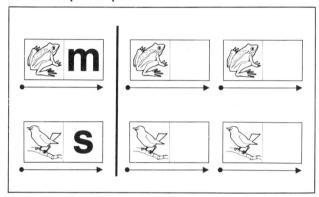

Take-Home 5

The exercise above shows the children that pairs such as **frog/m** can be repeated. Each time the pair appears, it must say **frog/m**.

Children cross out incorrect pairs.

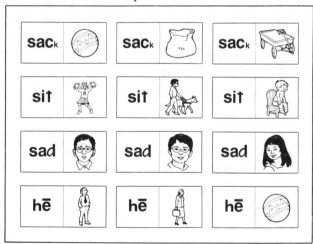

Take-Home 34

Children draw lines through sentences that do not apply, leaving the correct pair (the picture and one sentence).

Take-Home 61

Children connect the correct pairs.

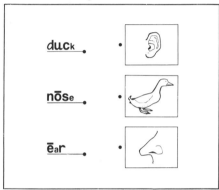

Take-Home 63

Reading Comprehension (Lessons 60-80)

The first written reading-comprehension items presented require the children to complete each sentence by circling the appropriate word.

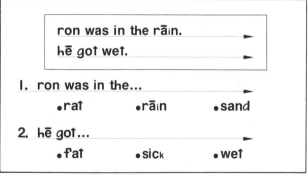

Take-Home 60

This format extends the skills mastered in the matching exercises, the sentence-saying exercises, and the comprehension exercises presented in connection with reading the story. In picture-completion items, starting at lesson 72, the children use their spelling and comprehension skills to complete two sentences for a given picture.

Fast Cycle II
(Lessons 81–170)

Sound Combinations

The first two sound combinations introduced in Fast Cycle II are **ar** and **al**. These combinations are followed by **ch, ea, ee, er, ing, oo, ou, qu, sh, th,** and **wh**. Below is an exercise from lesson 85 that reviews the combinations **ar** and **al** after both have been introduced.

TASK 2 Sound combination review

a. Here are some letters that go together. Get ready to tell me the sound they usually make.
b. Point to **ar**. What sound do these letters usually make? (Signal.) *Are.* Yes, **are**.
c. Repeat *b* with **al**.
d. Repeat both sound combinations until firm.

ar
al

Lesson 85

Critical Behaviors

1. In step *a*, describe the task to the children, telling them to get ready to tell the sound the letter combination makes.

2. In step *b*, point to **ar** and say, "What sound do these letters usually make?"

   - When pointing, hold your finger about an inch from the page, just below the middle of **ar**. Be careful not to cover parts of either sound.
   - Without moving your finger, say, "What sound do these letters usually make?"
   - Pause one second after you say the last word in your question (**make**).
   - Touch just below the middle of **ar**.

   - Touch under the sound combination for only an instant. (Use the same touching procedures you use for stop sounds.) Children are to say the sound combination **ar** quickly. They are not to drag it out.

3. Repeat step *b* of the format for the sound combination **al** (pronounced "all.")

   - Point to **al**. As you point, say, "What sound do these letters usually make?" Continue to point for one second.
   - Then touch just under the middle of **al**. Touch for only an instant. The children respond *all* the moment you touch under the combination.

Reading Vocabulary

In Fast Cycle II, the children read between twenty and forty-eight vocabulary words each day. Some of the reading-vocabulary formats are identical to those used in Fast Cycle I. Some require children to sound out the word first, and then identify it. Others require children to read words the fast way. Among the new formats introduced is the sound-combination format.

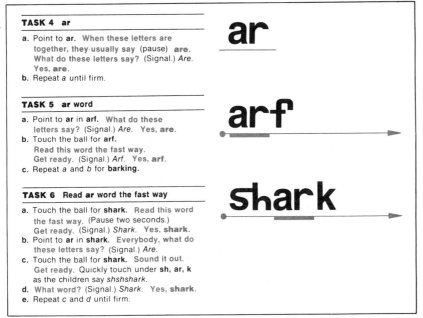

TASK 4 ar

a. Point to **ar**. When these letters are together, they usually say (pause) **are**. What do these letters say? (Signal.) *Are.* Yes, **are**.
b. Repeat *a* until firm.

TASK 5 ar word

a. Point to **ar** in **arf**. What do these letters say? (Signal.) *Are.* Yes, **are**.
b. Touch the ball for **arf**. Read this word the fast way. Get ready. (Signal.) *Arf.* Yes, **arf**.
c. Repeat *a* and *b* for **barking**.

TASK 6 Read ar word the fast way

a. Touch the ball for **shark**. Read this word the fast way. (Pause two seconds.) Get ready. (Signal.) *Shark.* Yes, **shark**.
b. Point to **ar** in **shark**. Everybody, what do these letters say? (Signal.) *Are.*
c. Touch the ball for **shark**. Sound it out. Get ready. Quickly touch under **sh, ar, k** as the children say *shshshark*.
d. What word? (Signal.) *Shark.* Yes, **shark**.
e. Repeat *c* and *d* until firm.

Lesson 81

Sound-Combination Formats

In lesson 81, the basic sound-combination format is introduced. The heading of the task indicates the sound combination involved: **ar**.

- In task 4, the teacher identifies what the letters say and tests the children: "What do these letters say?"
- In task 5, the teacher points to the bar that is under **ar** and asks, "What do these letters say?" The children then read the word the fast way.
- In task 6, the teacher tells the children to read the word the fast way; then to identify what the letters **ar** say; and finally to sound the word out and to answer the question, "What word?"

Critical Behaviors for Task 4

1. Point between **a** and **r** before you say, "When these letters are together, they usually say (pause) **are**."
2. Remember to pause before saying **are** in the above statement.
3. After you ask, "What do these letters say?" signal by touching just under the middle of **ar**.
4. Repeat step 3 until firm. Make sure that the children are pronouncing **are** appropriately.

Story Reading

In Fast Cycle II, sounding out is no longer used as a correction procedure in story reading. Correct all word-reading errors by telling the correct word or by calling on a child whose hand is raised. Direct the reader to return to the beginning of the sentence and reread the sentence. The correction procedure shown below is specified in all story-reading tasks.

To correct word-identification errors (**from**, for example)
1. That word is **from**. What word? *From.*
2. Go back to the beginning of the sentence and read the sentence again.

Lesson 81

Individual Checkouts for Rate and Accuracy

Instructions for checkouts specify which part of the story the child should read, in how many minutes, and the maximum number of acceptable errors (ranging from three to five). The last checkouts for the program (lessons 160, 165, and 170) specify a selection of 180 words to be read in two minutes with a maximum of five errors. This reading rate would be ninety words per minute.

For more information on individual checkouts, see page 44.

Read the Items

The teacher presentation for read-the-items exercises in Fast Cycle II is the same as that in Fast Cycle I. (See page 46.)

VOWEL MECHANICS
(Lessons 90–111)

In lessons 90 to 111, the focus of new teaching is on vowel mechanics. The following vowel mechanics activities take place:

1. The children are taught the names of the vowels: **a, e, i, o, u**.
2. The children learn to discriminate between short-vowel words (**mop**) and words that have a long vowel and a full-size final **e (mope)**.

Other activities that take place in this lesson range include the following:

1. The joined letters **th, sh**, and **ing** become disjoined.
2. The children are taught to identify the sound combination **ou**, and the combinations **th, sh**, and **ing** when the letters are disjoined.

3. Story-picture items are introduced in the take-homes.
4. Sentence-copying activities are dropped from the take-home activities (lesson 98).

Letter Names—Vowels
(Lessons 90–100)

The Letter Names track begins at lesson 90 and continues through lesson 100. (The track is resumed at lesson 114 and continues through lesson 125, during which time the children are taught alphabetical order, letter names for consonants, and capital letters.) The track contains three formats.

The letter-names activities are presented as the first tasks of the lesson (replacing sound-identification tasks). Shown below is the introductory format that appears in lesson 90. This format appears in two lessons.

LETTER NAMES

TASK 1 Listen, say vowel names

a. Point to the letters.
   You know the sounds for these letters. But these letters have names. I'll tell you the names of these letters. Listen.
   Touch each letter. Say the name:
   ā, ē, ī, ō, ū.
b. Say the names with me. Remember the **names** are what you said when these letters had lines over them.
c. Touch each letter. Say the names with the children.
d. Again. Repeat c until firm.
e. All by yourselves. Say the **names**.
   Point to each letter. (Pause.)
   The children respond.
f. Again. Repeat e until firm.

TASK 2 Say vowel names

a. Point to e. Everybody, what's the name of this letter? Get ready.
   Touch e. ē.
b. Point to o. Everybody, what's the name of this letter? Get ready.
   Touch o. ō.
c. Repeat a and b until firm.

a e i

o u

Lesson 90

Critical Behaviors for Task 1

1. Step *a* is a *model*. You touch each letter and say the name. Do not hold the name when you identify each letter. (Do not say āāā.) Say ā.
2. Step *b* is a *lead*. You touch each letter as the children say the name with you.
3. Step *e* is a *test*. You say, "All by yourselves. Say the **names**."

Critical Behaviors for Task 2

In task 2, you firm the names of two letters—**e** and **o**.

1. When presenting task 2, remember to give the children thinking time before you touch each letter.
2. Touch quickly, as you would touch a stop sound. The children are to respond by saying each name quickly—ē instead of ēēē.

Correction

If the children have trouble with this exercise, they are probably not firm on the preceding sounds lesson (which concentrated heavily on vowels, particularly vowels with lines over them). The best remedy might be to return to lesson 89 and repeat the sound-identification exercise. Then present lesson 90 again.

Track Development

After the introduction of letter names for the vowels in lessons 90 and 91, the children receive a daily review of letter names through lesson 100. When presenting these lessons, make sure that the children are firm on letter-name identification. They will use these letter names in the reading-vocabulary exercises.

Reading Vocabulary for Lessons 90–111

The major thrust of the Reading Vocabulary track in lessons 90 through 111 is to teach children how to read words such as **made** and **rode** that have a final **e** and a long-vowel sound and how to discriminate between these words and regularly spelled short-vowel words, such as **mad** and **rod**.

As letter names are being taught, the children are regularly presented with reading-vocabulary words that follow the long-**e** rule but that are written in Distar orthography:

This procedure strengthens identification of the words.

After letter names have been taught, the children are introduced to the rule about the final **e**. "If there is an **e** on the end of the word, you say the name of this letter" (pointing to the first vowel in the word). Note that the rule makes reference to the *name of this letter*, which is why the vowel names are taught before the words are introduced in reading vocabulary.

The children apply the rule about the final **e** to words that are presented with no lines over the vowel and a full-size **e**.

Teach the long-vowel-rule formats very carefully and present enough individual turns to give you feedback about how firm the children are. Beginning at lesson 107 and continuing throughout the program, children will read stories with many long-vowel patterns. If the long-vowel exercises have not been taught well, the lower-performing children may have difficulties.

Long-Vowel Rule

The first reading-vocabulary format that deals with the long-vowel rule appears in lesson 97.

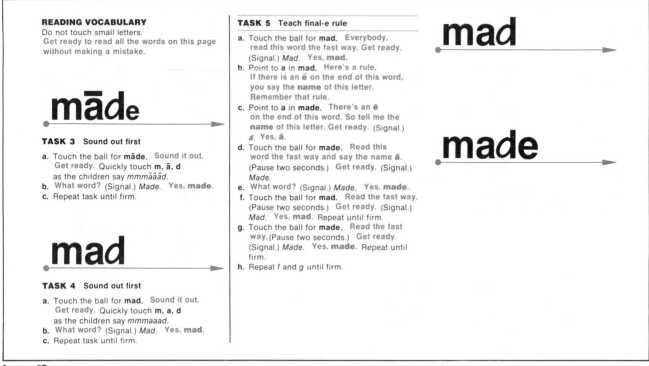

READING VOCABULARY
Do not touch small letters.
Get ready to read all the words on this page without making a mistake.

māde

TASK 3 Sound out first

a. Touch the ball for **māde**. Sound it out. Get ready. Quickly touch **m, ā, d** as the children say *mmmāāād*.
b. What word? (Signal.) *Made*. Yes, **made**.
c. Repeat task until firm.

mad

TASK 4 Sound out first

a. Touch the ball for **mad**. Sound it out. Get ready. Quickly touch **m, a, d** as the children say *mmmaaad*.
b. What word? (Signal.) *Mad*. Yes, **mad**.
c. Repeat task until firm.

TASK 5 Teach final-e rule

a. Touch the ball for **mad**. Everybody, read this word the fast way. Get ready. (Signal.) *Mad*. Yes, **mad**.
b. Point to **a** in **mad**. Here's a rule. If there is an **ē** on the end of this word, you say the **name** of this letter. Remember that rule.
c. Point to **a** in **made**. There's an **ē** on the end of this word. So tell me the **name** of this letter. Get ready. (Signal.) *ā*. Yes, **ā**.
d. Touch the ball for **made**. Read this word the fast way and say the name **ā**. (Pause two seconds.) Get ready. (Signal.) *Made*.
e. What word? (Signal.) *Made*. Yes, **made**.
f. Touch the ball for **mad**. Read the fast way. (Pause two seconds.) Get ready. (Signal.) *Mad*. Yes, **mad**. Repeat until firm.
g. Touch the ball for **made**. Read the fast way. (Pause two seconds.) Get ready. (Signal.) *Made*. Yes, **made**. Repeat until firm.
h. Repeat *f* and *g* until firm.

mad

made

Lesson 97

Note that two words are repeated on the page. In the first appearance of **made** (task 3), a long line and a small **e** are present. In the second appearance (task 5), there is no long line and the **e** is full-size.

- In step *b* of task 5 (titled **Teach final-e rule**), the teacher points to the **a** in **mad** and presents the rule about the final **e**: "If there is an **e** on the end of this word, you say the **name** of this letter."
- In step *c*, the teacher applies the rule to the word **made**. The teacher points to the **a** in **made** and tells the children, "There's an **e** on the end of this word. So tell me the **name** of this letter. Get ready." (Signal.)
- In step *d*, the children read the word the fast way, saying the name **ā**.
- In steps *f* and *g*, the children reread **mad** and **made** the fast way.

Critical Behaviors for Task 5

1. Fast pacing of the steps in this task is critical. In step *b*, remember to stress the word **name** in the rule. The discrimination between the *sound* and the *name* will be easier if you stress "You say the **name** of this letter."

PRACTICE saying the rule so that you can present it in step *b* without looking at the book. Say the rule as if it were important. (It is.)

2. In step *c*, present the rule in parts. Pause after you say, "There's an **ē** on the end of this word." If you wish, you can ask the children, "Do you see it?" Or even ask one of the children to touch it. Then say, "So tell me the **name** of this letter. Get ready." Signal by touching just under the **a**.

Corrections for Task 5

- In step *a*, if the children make mistakes on reading **mad**, use the standard sound-out correction. Then repeat step *a* of the format.

- In step *c*, the children may say the sound **ăăă**, not the name.

  To correct:

  1. Tell the children: **You said the sound. I want the name. What's the name?**
  2. Repeat steps *b* and *c* of the format.

- In step *d*, some children will make mistakes when trying to say the word (particularly the first time the format is presented).

  To correct:

  1. Immediately tell the children the word. **Made.**
  2. Relate the pronunciation to the rule. **I said** $\bar{a}$ **when I read the word. Listen:** *māāāāāde.* **Hear the** $\bar{a}$?
  3. Repeat steps *c* and *d* of the format until firm.

- In step *f*, the children may make mistakes. They may read **mad** as **made**.

  To correct:

  1. First use the standard sound-it-out, what-word correction.
  2. Present step *g* for the word **made**.
  3. Then repeat steps *f* and *g* until the children are quite firm on both words.

PRACTICE presenting the format and the corrections in steps *c*, *d*, and *f*. Work with another adult, who makes the mistakes. Work on the corrections until you can execute them without referring to the format.

Practice Final-e Rule (Lesson 99)

Vowel-rule exercises similar to the one above are presented in lessons 97 and 98. In lesson 99, the children are introduced to a format that requires less teacher prompting. The format from lesson 100 is shown below.

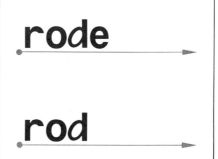

TASK 6 Practice final-e rule

a. Touch the ball for **rode.** Everybody, is there an **ē** on the end of this word? (Signal.) *Yes.*

b. Point to **o** in **rode.** So tell me what you say for this letter. (Signal.) *ō.*

c. Touch the ball for **rode.** Everybody, read this word the fast way and remember to say **ō.** Get ready. (Signal.) *Rode.* Yes, **rode.**

d. Touch the ball for **rod.** Everybody, is there an **ē** on the end of this word? (Signal.) *No.*

e. Point to **o** in **rod.** So tell me what you say for this letter. (Signal.) *ooo.*

f. Touch the ball for **rod.** Everybody, read this word the fast way and remember to say **ooo.** Get ready. (Signal.) *Rod.* Yes, **rod.**

g. Repeat *a* through *f* until firm.

Lesson 100

Long-Vowel Words, Short-Vowel Words

In lesson 102, a new vowel-rule format is introduced. This format involves a column of long-vowel words, a column of short-vowel words, and a column of short- and long-vowel words.

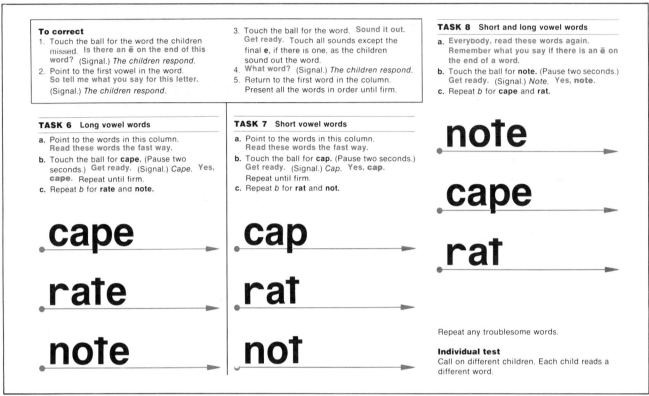

To correct
1. Touch the ball for the word the children missed. Is there an ē on the end of this word? (Signal.) *The children respond.*
2. Point to the first vowel in the word. So tell me what you say for this letter. (Signal.) *The children respond.*

3. Touch the ball for the word. Sound it out. Get ready. Touch all sounds except the final **e**, if there is one, as the children sound out the word.
4. What word? (Signal.) *The children respond.*
5. Return to the first word in the column. Present all the words in order until firm.

TASK 6   Long vowel words
a. Point to the words in this column. Read these words the fast way.
b. Touch the ball for **cape.** (Pause two seconds.) Get ready. (Signal.) *Cape.* Yes, **cape.** Repeat until firm.
c. Repeat *b* for **rate** and **note.**

TASK 7   Short vowel words
a. Point to the words in this column. Read these words the fast way.
b. Touch the ball for **cap.** (Pause two seconds.) Get ready. (Signal.) *Cap.* Yes, **cap.** Repeat until firm.
c. Repeat *b* for **rat** and **not.**

TASK 8   Short and long vowel words
a. Everybody, read these words again. Remember what you say if there is an ē on the end of a word.
b. Touch the ball for **note.** (Pause two seconds.) Get ready. (Signal.) *Note.* Yes, **note.**
c. Repeat *b* for **cape** and **rat.**

Repeat any troublesome words.

Individual test
Call on different children. Each child reads a different word.

Lesson 102

Corrections

The correction procedure for all words is specified in the box on the format page.

PRACTICE the correction in the box in the format above. Note that step 3 of the correction involves sounding out the misidentified word. When sounding out words that have a final **e**, *you do not touch the final e.* If the children are to sound out the word **cape**, you touch **c, a,** and **p.** In the word **note**, you touch **n, o,** and **t.** Practice the correction with these words.

- Expect the children to have trouble with task 8, in which they read both long- and short-vowel words. You can reduce errors by pausing at least two seconds before saying "Get ready" and signaling.
- If the children make errors on any word, correct them. Then return to task 6 and present tasks 6, 7, and 8 until the children are perfectly firm.

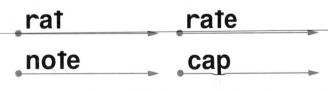

Disjoining Joined Letters

At lesson 107, the joined letters **th** and **ing** become disjoined. At lesson 110, **sh** is disjoined. All other joined letters are disjoined at lesson 112, when traditional print replaces the Distar orthography.

Shown below is the format that introduces the disjoined letters **ing**.

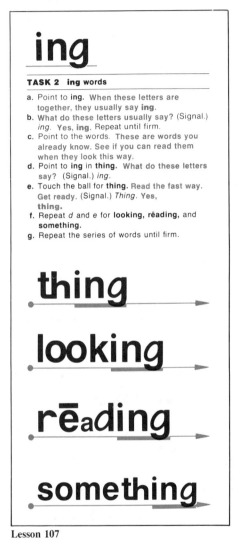

Lesson 107

Critical Behaviors

1. In step *a*, show the children the disjoined **ing** and tell them that the letters say **ing**.
2. In step *c*, point to the familiar words and tell the children that they are going to read them with a disjoined **ing**.

3. Steps *d* and *e* are repeated for each word. In *d*, point to the **ing** and say, "What do these letters say?" Signal by touching under the middle of **ing**. Do not slash.
4. In step *e*, touch the ball and say, "Read the fast way. Get ready." Signal by slashing right.

PRACTICE steps *d* and *e* for each of the words on the page.

Sample: For the word **thing**, point just under **ing**. Say, "What do these letters say?" Signal by touching just under the middle of **ing**. Touch the ball for **thing**. "Read the fast way. Get ready." Signal by slashing right.

Corrections

In step *d*, the children may say *thing* instead of *ing*.

To correct:

1. Cover **th** and point to **ing**.
2. Ask: What do *these* letters say? Signal by touching under **ing**.
3. Uncover **th**. Let's do it again. Point to **ing**. What do these letters say?
4. Continue to step *e*.

Correcting words with unjoined letters:

If the children misidentify any word in the list, correct in this way.

1. Point to **ing**. What do these letters say?
2. Touch the ball for the word. Sound it out. Get ready. Move under **ing**. Then touch the remaining full-size letters or joined sounds.
3. When the sounding out is firm, ask: What word?
4. Return to the word **thing** and repeat *e* and *f* in the format for each word.

Samples:

Word	Children sound out	What word?
thing	thththiiing	thing
looking	lllooooookiiing	looking
rēₐding	rrrēēēdiiing	reading

PRACTICE the sound-out correction with the following words. You will use this correction to correct mistakes on all words with letters that become disjoined.

Correction for **shed**

1. Point to **sh**. What do these letters say? Touch under the middle of **sh**. The children respond, *shshsh*.
2. Touch the ball of the arrow. Sound it out. Get ready. Move under **sh, e, d** as the children say, *shshsheeed*.
3. Return to the ball of the arrow. What word? Slash right. The children respond, *shed*. Yes, *shed*.

Correction for **ther**e

1. Point to **th**. What do these letters say? Touch under the middle of **th**. The children respond, *thththth*.
2. Touch the ball of the arrow. Sound it out. Get ready. Move under **th, e, r** as the children say, *thththeeerrr*.
3. Return to the ball. What word? Slash right. The children respond, *there*. Yes, *there*.

---

*Correcting words with taught sound combinations and **ed** endings:*

Correction for **call**ed

1. Cover the **ed** ending. Point to **al** in **called**. What do these letters say? The children respond, *all*. Yes, *all*.
2. Touch the ball of the arrow. Sound it out. Get ready.
3. Move under **c, al**. The children say, *call*.
4. Return to the ball. What does the first part say? Slash right. The children respond, *call*. Yes, *call*.
5. Uncover the **ed** ending. Touch the ball of the arrow. What does it say now? Slash right. The children pronounce the word as it is normally pronounced, *calld*. Yes, *called*.

PRACTICE the correction with the words below. The underscored parts show you what to point to first. (The words you are working with in the teacher-presentation materials may not be underscored.)

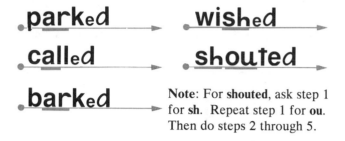

Note: For **shouted**, ask step 1 for **sh**. Repeat step 1 for **ou**. Then do steps 2 through 5.

---

*Correcting irregular words with **ed** endings:*

If a word is irregular, direct the children to sound out and identify the word as it would appear without an ending. Then uncover the ending.

Correction for **moved**

For the word **moved**, cover only the **d**. Direct the children to sound out *mmmooovvveee* and identify the first part (*move*). Then uncover the **d** and ask, What does it say now?

PRACTICE this correction for the word *loved*.

Correction for **touch**ed

For the word **touched**, cover the **ed** and have the children sound out and identify **touch**. Then uncover the **ed** and ask, What does it say now?

PRACTICE this correction for the words *wanted* and *watched*.

Long- and Short-Vowel Words

In lesson 119 the discrimination of long-vowel and short-vowel words is introduced. Earlier in the program, the pronunciation of these words was cued by the Distar orthography (which has a macron over the vowel if the vowel is long). Beginning with lesson 119, the children discriminate between word pairs like **moping** and **mopping.**

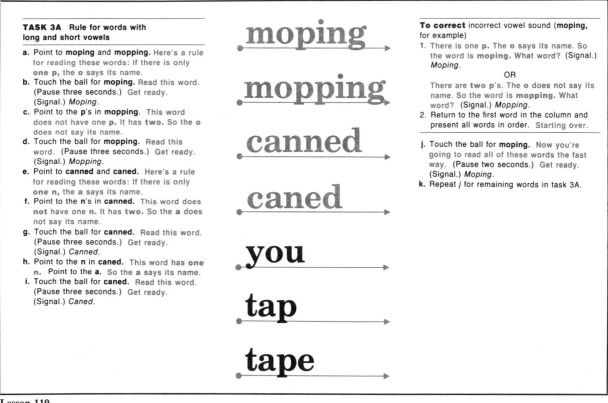

TASK 3A   Rule for words with long and short vowels

a. Point to **moping** and **mopping.** Here's a rule for reading these words: If there is only **one p,** the **o** says its name.
b. Touch the ball for **moping.** Read this word. (Pause three seconds.) Get ready. (Signal.) *Moping.*
c. Point to the **p's** in **mopping.** This word does not have one **p.** It has **two.** So the **o** does not say its name.
d. Touch the ball for **mopping.** Read this word. (Pause three seconds.) Get ready. (Signal.) *Mopping.*
e. Point to **canned** and **caned.** Here's a rule for reading these words: If there is only **one n,** the **a** says its name.
f. Point to the **n's** in **canned.** This word does **not** have one **n.** It has **two.** So the **a** does not say its name.
g. Touch the ball for **canned.** Read this word. (Pause three seconds.) Get ready. (Signal.) *Canned.*
h. Point to the **n** in **caned.** This word has **one n.** Point to the **a.** So the **a** says its name.
i. Touch the ball for **caned.** Read this word. (Pause three seconds.) Get ready. (Signal.) *Caned.*

To correct incorrect vowel sound (**moping,** for example)
1. There is one **p.** The **o** says its name. So the word is **moping.** What word? (Signal.) *Moping.*

OR

There are **two p's.** The **o** does not say its name. So the word is **mopping.** What word? (Signal.) *Mopping.*
2. Return to the first word in the column and present all words in order. Starting over.

j. Touch the ball for **moping.** Now you're going to read all of these words the fast way. (Pause two seconds.) Get ready. (Signal.) *Moping.*
k. Repeat *j* for remaining words in task 3A.

moping

mopping

canned

caned

you

tap

tape

Lesson 119

Practice the entire format and the correction procedure. Directed application of the procedure appears in the program for eight lessons. Use this procedure to correct any mistakes on long- and short-vowel words of this type in word lists for the remainder of the program. To correct the word **caned,** for instance, tell the children: There is one *n.* The *a* says its name. So the word is *caned.* What word? Then make sure that you return to the first word in the column and present all words in order. If you follow this step, the children will learn the discrimination with few errors.

Take-Homes for Lessons 90–111

The following activities appear on the daily take-homes:

- Story Items
- Reading Comprehension
- Following Instructions—Type 1, lessons 90–96; Type 2, lessons 97–111
- Sentence Copying—which stops at lesson 97
- Story-Picture Items—introduced in lesson 107

There are teacher-directed take-home activities in only a few lessons. The children work nearly all of the activities independently. A major emphasis of the take-home activities in this lesson range is on the children's writing word responses to comprehension items.

Following Instructions (Lesson 90)

The first activity that deals with word writing is the following-instructions exercise in lesson 90. The teacher presentation and the children's activity for that exercise are shown here.

TASK 22 Box and circle items

Children call letters by sounds, not letter names.
a. Pass out Take-Home 90 to each child.
b. Point to the first circle on side 1.
Everybody, touch this circle.
Check children's responses.
c. Everybody, touch instruction 1 next to the circle.
d. Reading the fast way. First word.
Check children's responses. Get ready.
Clap for each word as the children read:
Make the word **sun** *in the circle.*
e. What does this instruction tell you to do?
(Signal.) *Make the word* **sun** *in the circle.*

To correct
Tell the children the answer.
Then repeat *d* and *e*.

---

f. Everybody, get ready to read instruction 2 next to the circle. First word.
Check children's responses. Get ready.
Clap for each word as the children read:
Make the word **cat** *under the circle.*
g. What does this instruction tell you to do?
(Signal.) *Make the word* **cat** *under the circle.*
h. Point to the instructions. Everybody, read the instructions to yourselves. Then do what the instructions tell you to do.
Check children's responses.
i. You'll follow the instructions for the other circle later.

Lesson 90

---

1. mãke the word sun in the circle.

2. mãke the word cat under the circle.

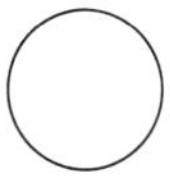

Take-Home 90

If the children are firm on the preceding following-instructions tasks, they should have no trouble with this exercise. The teacher instructions appear only in lessons 90 and 91. It is a good idea to watch the children as they work the following-instructions exercises in lessons 92 and 93. If the children ask how to work the exercises, *do not tell them.* Instead, instruct them to read the instructions aloud. Then say, "Do what those instructions tell you to do."

In lesson 97, variations of instructions are introduced for three take-home activities: following instructions, reading comprehension, and story items.

Following Instructions (Lesson 97)

The teacher presentation and the children's material for the new following-instructions activity are shown below.

TASK 19 Read sentence, follow instructions

a. Pass out Take-Home 97 to each child.
b. Point to the sentence in the first box on side 1.
c. Everybody, touch this sentence on your take-home. Check children's responses.
d. Everybody, read the sentence in the box. First word. Get ready. Clap for each word as the children read: *Three men sat in a car.*
e. Everybody, say that sentence without looking. (Signal.) *Three men sat in a car.* Repeat until firm.
f. Touch instruction 1 below the sentence in the box. Check children's responses.
g. Read that instruction. First word. Get ready. Clap for each word as the children read: *Circle the word car.*
h. What are you going to do? (Signal.) *Circle the word* **car.**
i. You're going to circle the word **car.** Everybody, touch the word **car.** Check children's responses.
j. What are you going to do to the word **car?** (Signal.) *Circle it.*

To correct
1. Have the children read instruction 1 below the box.
2. Then ask, What are you going to do to the word **car?**

---

k. Everybody, touch instruction 2 below the sentence in the box. Check children's responses.
l. Read that instruction. First word. Get ready. Clap for each word as the children read: *Make a line over the word men.*
m. What are you going to do? (Signal.) *Make a line over the word* **men.**
n. You're going to make a line over the word **men.** Everybody, touch the word **men** in the box. Check children's responses.
o. What are you going to do to the word **men?** (Signal.) *Make a line over it.*

To correct
1. Have the children read instruction 2 below the box.
2. Then ask, What are you going to do to the word **men?**

---

p. Everybody, read instruction 1 to yourself and do what it tells you to do. Check children's responses.
q. Everybody, read instruction 2 to yourself and do what it tells you to do. Check children's responses.
r. Everybody, you'll follow the instructions for the other sentence later.

Lesson 97

three men sat in a car.

1. circle the word car.

2. māke a līne ōver the word men.

---

her nāme was nell.

1. māke a līne under the word her.

2. māke a līne ōver the word nell.

PRACTICE presenting the format and the corrections that are specified. If the children have mechanical troubles (finding the items under the box, finding the words in the box), repeat the task after correcting the mistakes.

If the children make mistakes on the items for the first following-instructions sentence, structure the presentation on the second sentence. The structured teacher presentation runs for only one lesson. During this lesson, make the children as firm as possible.

Reading Comprehension (Lesson 97)

Also in lesson 97, the children begin writing responses to reading-comprehension items. (In earlier reading-comprehension tasks, the children had merely circled the answers.) The children's material and the teacher presentation for the reading-comprehension exercise from lesson 97 are shown below.

a little shark was trȳing to swim. a fish
cāme up and asked, "can I give you a hand?"
the shark said, "fish dōn't have hands.
they have fins."

1. the fish asked if he could give the

   shark a _____.   • hand   • trick   • fish

2. do fish have hands? _____   • yes   • no

TASK 20 Read story, answer items

a. Hold up side 2 of your take-home.
b. Point to the first story. Everybody, touch this story on your take-home. Check children's responses.
c. Read the fast way. First word. Check children's responses. Get ready. Clap. *A.*
d. Next word. Check children's responses. Get ready. Clap. *Little.*
e. Repeat *d* for the remaining words in the story.
f. Let's do the items for that story. From now on, you're going to write your answers in the blanks. Don't circle the answers. Just write them in the blanks.
g. Everybody, read item 1. First word. Check children's responses. Get ready. Clap for each word as the children read: *The fish asked if he could give the shark a. . . .*
h. Everybody, what's the answer? (Signal.) *Hand.*
i. Write the answer in the blank. Check children's responses.
j. Everybody, read item 2. First word. Check children's responses. Get ready. Clap for each word as the children read: *Do fish have hands?*
k. What's the answer? (Signal.) *No.*
l. Write that answer in the blank. Check children's responses.

Note that in the children's material, the blanks are open to provide space for the children to write the answers.

- In steps *c* through *e* of the teacher-presentation format, the children read the story about the little fish.
- In step *f*, the teacher tells them that they will write answers in the blanks.
- In step *g*, the children read item 1. *The fish asked if he could give the shark a _____.*
- In step *h*, the children answer the question.
- In step *i*, they write the answer in the blank.
- In steps *j* through *l*, they do item 2 with the teacher.

This is the only lesson in which the children receive the structured instructions. In following lessons, they are to work on their own. It is therefore important to make sure that the children are firmed in lesson 97. If they are not, monitor their reading-comprehension work in lessons 98 and 99.

Story Items (Lesson 97)

In lesson 97, the story items are changed so that the children respond by writing answers in the blanks, not by circling answers. The reading comprehension and the story items follow the same form. There are blanks in every item. The children write the appropriate answers in the blanks.

The teacher presentation and the story-items exercise for lesson 97 are shown below.

TASK 22 Story items

Point to the story-items exercise. Today you're going to write the answers in the blanks. Remember, don't circle them. Write them.

Lesson 97

---

1. what is the name of the cow in this story?

   _____
   • walter   • moo   • carmen

2. carmen has a very _____ moo.
   • loud   • little   • fast

3. where did the children go? _____
   • to the store   • to the farm   • to the lot

4. they came to _____ cows.
   • see   • pet   • hit

5. one child fell _____.
   • in a box   • in a hole   • in a creek

Take-Home 97

If possible, monitor the children when they work the story items in lesson 97. If they circle items, show them the blanks and say, "These blanks are open so that you can write in them. That's what you're supposed to do. Find the right answer and write it in the blank."

Spelling Conventions for Reading Comprehension and Story Items

In some of the take-home activities, the children must compose the answers (not copy them). Follow these rules with regard to their spelling of words:

1. If the word has occurred in the spelling program, the children should be held accountable for spelling it accurately.
2. If the word appears in the choices that are presented with the item, the children should spell the word accurately.
3. The words **yes** and **no** are to be spelled accurately.
4. If the word is in the reading-comprehension story, the children should find the word and spell it accurately.
5. If the item involves writing words that are not on the take-home and that have not been presented in the spelling program, do not expect the children to spell all words accurately. Accept phonetic spelling.

Correcting Spelling Mistakes

If the misspelled word occurs in the reading-comprehension activity, follow this correction:

1. Ask the child to identify the misspelled word.
2. Say: Find the word in the story.
3. After the child finds the word, say: Now write the word the way it is written in the story.

If the misspelled word is one that occurred earlier in the spelling program, have the child spell the word, following the spelling program format shown below. Then have the child write the word.

1. *(Model)* Say, Here are the sounds in the word *stop*. Listen. sss (pause) *t* (pause) *ooo* (pause) *p*.
2. *(Test)* Write the word.

When spelling-by-letter-names begins, use the same correction procedure (model, test) but refer to *letter names* instead of *sounds*.

Following Instructions (Lesson 97)

A new type of following-instructions exercise begins in lesson 97 and continues through lesson 144. These exercises present a sentence in a box. Expect some children to have trouble with this type of item. Below is the following-instructions exercise from lesson 107.

```
┌─────────────────────────────────────────┐
│        ┌──────────────────────┐          │
│        │ tim went to the park. │         │
│        └──────────────────────┘          │
│                                          │
│  1. circle the word that tells who went to the park.  │
│                                          │
│  2. make a line over the words that tell where tim went.  │
│                                          │
│  3. make a line over the circle.         │
└─────────────────────────────────────────┘
```

Take-Home 107

Mistake (item 1): Some children circle the word **park**.

Correction

1. Have the children read the sentence in the box aloud.
2. Ask the question: **Who went to the park?**
3. Have the children read item 1 aloud. *Circle the word that tells who went to the park.*
4. Say: **Show me the right word in the box.** The children show you the word **Tim.** **Yes,** *Tim.* **Read the item to yourself and figure out what you're going to do to the word** *Tim* **.... Do it.**

Monitor the children's performance. If you note that they are having trouble with "who" questions, correct the errors. Don't let errors accumulate for days.

Mistake (item 2): Some children make a line over the word **park**.

Correction

1. Have the children read the sentence in the box aloud.
2. Ask the question: **Where** ░░ ░ **go?**
3. Have the children read item 2 aloud. *Make a line over the words that tell where Tim went.*
4. Say: **Show me the right words in the box.** The children show you the words **to the park.** **Yes,** *to the park*.
5. Have the children read the item to themselves and do what the item tells them.

Again, monitor the children's performance and correct errors as soon as they appear.

Story-Picture Items

The Story-Picture Items track begins in lesson 107. It sets the stage for picture deductions.

Story-picture-items activities involve questions similar to those presented in the picture-comprehension activities that are introduced every day after the story has been read.

The teacher-presentation format and the story-picture items from lesson 107 are shown below.

```
┌─────────────────────────────────────────┐
│ TASK 12  Story picture                   │
│  a. Pass out Take-Home 107 to each child.│
│  b. Point to the story-picture items exercise on │
│     side 2.                              │
│  c. Here's something new on your take-home │
│     today. Everybody, touch the instructions. │
│     Check children's responses.          │
│  d. My turn to read the fast way. Read: Look │
│     at the picture on page 76 of your reader. │
│  e. Your turn to read the instructions the fast │
│     way. First word. Check children's    │
│     responses. Get ready. Clap for each word │
│     as the children read: Look at the picture on │
│     page 76 of your reader.              │
│  f. Everybody, what do the instructions tell │
│     you to do? (Signal.) Look at the picture on │
│     page 76 of my reader. Do it. Check that │
│     the children look at the picture on page 76. │
│  g. Everybody, touch item 1 below the    │
│     instructions on your take-home. Check │
│     children's responses.                │
│  h. Read the fast way. First word. Check │
│     children's responses. Get ready. Clap for │
│     each word as the children read: Is Sam │
│     reading a paper?                     │
│  i. Look at the picture on page 76. Is Sam │
│     reading a paper? (Signal.) Yes. Yes, he │
│     is reading a paper.                  │
│  j. Write the answer in the blank. Check │
│     children's responses.                │
│  k. Everybody, you'll write the answer to the │
│     other question later.                │
└─────────────────────────────────────────┘
```

Lesson 107

```
┌─────────────────────────────────────────┐
│  look at the picture on page 76 of your reader. │
│                                          │
│  1. is sam reading a paper? _____    │
│                                          │
│  2. do you see sam's toy car? _____  │
└─────────────────────────────────────────┘
```

Take-Home 107

TEXTBOOK PREPARATION
(Lessons 112–170)

In lessons 112 to 170, the following major activities occur:

1. The children are taught the letter names and the alphabet.
2. The children are taught to identify capital letters.
3. All joined letters become disjoined.
4. The children are taught to identify the sound combination **ea**.
5. Traditional textbook print starts in the reading vocabulary at lesson 112. By lesson 123, all stories and take-homes are written in traditional orthography (no joined letters, small letters, or long lines over the vowels), and capital letters appear where appropriate.
6. New tracks occur in the take-homes:
   Story-Items Review (lessons 127-157)
   Picture Deductions (lessons 126-157)
   Written Deductions Type 1 (lessons 147-157)
   Written Deductions Type 2 (lessons l58-170)
   Reading Comprehension of Factual
      Information (lessons 151-170)

Letter Names and Capital Letters

In a series of exercises from lessons 114 to 125, the letter names for vowels are reviewed, alphabetical order (using lowercase letters) is taught, and capital letters are introduced.

Letter Names

All lowercase and capital letters are taught by name, not by sound. Letter-names exercises begin in lesson 114 and continue through lesson 117. The track contains three formats. The format for letter names and alphabetical order that appears in lesson 114 is shown here.

Critical Behaviors

The most critical behavior in presenting this format is your timing. The task will be new for some children, but other children will already know the letter names. They will want to rush ahead and say the names quickly.

A good timing when you test the children in step *f* is about one letter name per second.

1. First point to the letter; then touch it.
2. When you touch the letter, the children are to respond.
3. Immediately release your touch.

The children should not hold the name. For example, they should not say *effffff*; they should say *ef*.

TASK 1   Letter names

a. Use acetate and crayon.
b. Look at these letters. You know the names of the letters that are in red. Get ready to tell me those letter names.
c. Point under **a**. Get ready. Tap. *a.*
d. Repeat step c for **e, i, o,** and **u.**
e. My turn to say the names of all the letters. Point to each letter and say its name.
f. Your turn. See how many letter names you can say. Point under **a.** Get ready. Tap. *a.* Tap under each remaining letter as the children say its name.

To correct
1. Immediately say the letter name.
2. What name? Tap. *The children respond.*
3. Circle the letter.
4. Continue to the next letter.

g. If any letters are circled, say: Everybody, get ready to tell me the names of all the circled letters. Point to each circled letter. Get ready. Tap. *The children respond.*

Individual test

a. See how many letter names you can say.
b. Call on different children. Immediately say the correct letter name if the child makes a mistake.

---

abcdefghijklmnopqrstuvwxyz

Lesson 114

In lessons 116 and 117, the letters presented are not in alphabetical order. The children identify each letter.

Capital Letters

Two formats are used to teach the capital letters. One format presents the "easy" capitals; the other presents the "hard" capitals. Easy capital letters are those that closely resemble their lowercase counterparts. Hard capitals (**A, R, D, E, Q, B, L, H, G**) don't resemble their lowercase counterparts.

Introducing Easy Capitals (Lessons 118–120)

The sixteen "easy" capitals appear in random order in a row on the page. The teacher says, "Capital letters are bigger than the other letters. In a few days, every sentence that you'll read will begin with a capital letter."

Introducing Hard Capitals (Lessons 120–125)

The "hard" capitals are introduced in two groups. Shown below is the first group (**A, R, D, E, Q**), introduced in lesson 120. The letters appear with their lowercase counterparts for one lesson; then they are reviewed in random order without their lowercase counterparts.

TASK 2 Introducing hard capitals

a. These are capital letters that don't look like the letters you know. The letters you know are in the top row. The capitals are in the row below.
b. Point under capital **A**. This is capital A.
c. Repeat step *b* for each remaining capital.
d. Your turn. Point under capital **A**. What capital? (Signal.) *A.*
e. Repeat step *d* for each remaining capital.
f. Repeat steps *d* and *e* until firm.

a r d e q
A R D E Q

Lesson 120

The same steps are followed for the second group (**B, L, H, C**). In the final format for hard capitals, all the hard capitals are mixed.

By lesson 123, all sentences and stories in the storybook and on the take-homes follow traditional rules for capitalization.

Reading Vocabulary for Lessons 112–170

Reading vocabulary is the second activity scheduled in lessons 114 to 125 (following letter-names or capital-letters tasks). In lessons 126 to 170, it is scheduled as the first activity.

During lesson range 112 to 170, four word-attack procedures are introduced in reading vocabulary:

1. Reading the fast way without sounding out
2. Reading words that have an underlined part by first reading the underlined part; then reading the whole word the fast way
3. Reading a word the fast way; then spelling the word
4. Spelling a word; then reading it the fast way

Each reading-vocabulary exercise presents four or five columns of words (seven words in a column). All words in a particular column are treated in a particular way. Some columns have words with underlined parts; some have words that are to be read and then spelled. Because each lesson presents between twenty-eight and thirty-six words, the teaching of the reading-vocabulary exercises must be fast-paced, with the emphasis on *reading*, and reading accurately.

Time Frame for Reading Vocabulary

Your goal should be to complete the reading-vocabulary part of the lesson in no more than ten minutes. Within this time, a group that is firm can read all the columns of words and take individual turns reading a column.

If the children in a group are not firm at lesson 112, the reading-vocabulary part of the lesson may take fifteen minutes. Here are some suggestions for improving the children's performance:

1. Enforce the criterion specified on the page. Be encouraging, but be firm. Praise the children for working hard.

2. Use the specified correction procedure, always returning to the first word in the column and repeating the column.

3. If most mistakes are made by the same children, and if those children cannot be moved to a group that is placed at an earlier lesson, give more individual turns, particularly on columns on which the children were very firm during group reading. Don't rush the children; praise accuracy.

4. Present a time challenge to the group. "You're all reading with very few mistakes, just like the big children. Let's see if you can do all the words on these pages in _____ minutes." Time the group. Offer an incentive. For lower-performing groups, first limit your challenge to accurately reading one column. "This column is hard. Let's see if you can read the whole column without making more than two mistakes." Gradually increase your performance expectation until the group can read all the words in ten minutes or less. Groups that are firm find this part of the lesson very reinforcing, especially when they are timed.

5. Pace your presentation appropriately. Note how fast individuals in the group perform on column reading. Use this information to adjust the rate at which you present words to the group. Also note the children's story-reading rate. There should be no great discrepancies between the rate at which the children read in the reading-vocabulary exercises and their story-reading rate, although the reading-vocabulary rate will be slightly slower. If there are great discrepancies (reasonable story-reading rate and very slow, drony reading-vocabulary performance), the children don't really understand that you want the same reading behavior on reading vocabulary as on story reading. Use challenges to clarify your expectations.

6. Remember to wait until the end of the reading-vocabulary part of the lesson to give individual turns.

Note: If your group is large, not all children will get a turn to read a column each day. In this situation, be sure to call on the lower-performing children more frequently than on the higher performers.

Correction Procedure (Lessons 112–121)

Starting at lesson 122, you will use a spelling correction for all reading-vocabulary errors. However, in lessons 112 to 121 (before the children are firm on letter names) use the correction procedure shown below. You identify the correct word; the children identify the word; then you return to the first word in the column and present all words in order.

> **To correct** word-identification errors (**cone,** for example)
> 1. That word is **cone.** What word? (Signal.) *Cone.*
> 2. Return to the first word in the column and present all words in order. Starting over.

Lesson 112

Spelling by Letter Names

All letter names are taught by lesson 117. Starting with lesson 117, the children apply their spelling skills to words they read. Spelling improves word identification because spelling forces attention to every letter in a word. In all spelling formats, the teacher signals by tapping under each letter in the word.

TASK 3   Spelling by letter names

a. My turn to spell some of these words by saying the letter names.

b. Touch the ball for **gave.** My turn.   Tap under each letter as you say, **g·a·v·e.**

c. Touch the ball for **here.** My turn.   Tap under each letter as you say, **h·e·r·e.**

d. Touch the ball for **when.** My turn.   Tap under each letter as you say, **w·h·e·n.**

e. Your turn to spell all the words in this column by letter names.

f. Touch the ball for **gave.** Spell by letter names. Get ready.   Tap under each letter as children say **g·a·v·e.**

g. Repeat step *f* for each remaining word in the column.

h. Repeat any words on which children make mistakes.

i. Now you're going to read all the words in this column the fast way.

j. Touch the ball for **gave.** Get ready.   Slash. *Gave.*

k. Repeat step *j* for each remaining word in the column.

l. Repeat steps *j* and *k* until firm.

gave

here

when

bug

because

doing

came

Lesson 117

Children Spell, Then Read
(Lessons 119–170)

The words in this format are familiar. They have usually been presented several times in other formats. Children spell each word and then read it.

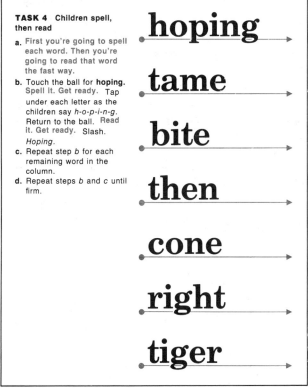

TASK 4 Children spell, then read

a. First you're going to spell each word. Then you're going to read that word the fast way.
b. Touch the ball for **hoping**. Spell it. Get ready. Tap under each letter as the children say *h-o-p-i-n-g*. Return to the ball. Read it. Get ready. Slash. *Hoping.*
c. Repeat step *b* for each remaining word in the column.
d. Repeat steps *b* and *c* until firm.

hoping
tame
bite
then
cone
right
tiger

Lesson 126

Words Beginning with Capital Letters
(Lessons 122–125)

Each word in the column begins with a capital letter. Children do not say "capital" when they spell words with capital letters. For example, they spell the word **Ann,** *a-n-n* (not *"capital" a-n-n*). After lesson 125, words with capitals are mixed in with words that begin with lowercase letters.

Teacher Reads the Words in Red
(Lessons 112–170)

Some words in the column are red; some are black. The red words are usually new or difficult words. The teacher first identifies the red words; then the children spell them (steps *a* through *d* of the format from lesson 126 shown below). In the last part of the format (steps *e* through *h*), the children return to the first word in the column and read all the words.

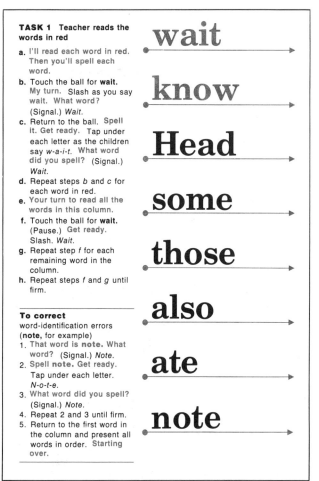

TASK 1 Teacher reads the words in red

a. I'll read each word in red. Then you'll spell each word.
b. Touch the ball for **wait**. My turn. Slash as you say wait. What word? (Signal.) *Wait.*
c. Return to the ball. Spell it. Get ready. Tap under each letter as the children say *w-a-i-t*. What word did you spell? (Signal.) *Wait.*
d. Repeat steps *b* and *c* for each word in red.
e. Your turn to read all the words in this column.
f. Touch the ball for **wait**. (Pause.) Get ready. Slash. *Wait.*
g. Repeat step *f* for each remaining word in the column.
h. Repeat steps *f* and *g* until firm.

To correct
word-identification errors (**note,** for example)
1. That word is **note.** What word? (Signal.) *Note.*
2. Spell **note.** Get ready. Tap under each letter. *N-o-t-e.*
3. What word did you spell? (Signal.) *Note.*
4. Repeat 2 and 3 until firm.
5. Return to the first word in the column and present all words in order. Starting over.

wait
know
Head
some
those
also
ate
note

Lesson 126

Words with Underlined Parts
(Lessons 112–170)

At least one column of words in every lesson presents words with underlined parts. Children read the underlined part; then they read the whole word. This procedure is used for many types of words: compound words (**may<u>be</u>, him<u>self</u>, some<u>body</u>, some<u>body</u>**); words with sound combinations (**th<u>em</u>, l<u>eave</u>, sh<u>out</u>** or **sh<u>ou</u>t**); words that follow the long-vowel rule with endings (**hop<u>ed</u>, hop<u>ped</u>, tap<u>ed</u>**); and words with various endings (**dim<u>es</u>, start<u>ing</u>, we'<u>ll</u>, clos<u>er</u>, dress<u>ed</u>, poor<u>est</u>**).

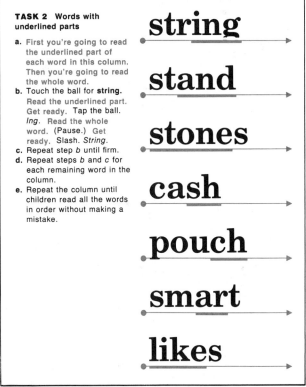

TASK 2 Words with underlined parts

a. First you're going to read the underlined part of each word in this column. Then you're going to read the whole word.
b. Touch the ball for **string**. Read the underlined part. Get ready. Tap the ball. *Ing.* Read the whole word. (Pause.) Get ready. Slash. *String.*
c. Repeat step *b* until firm.
d. Repeat steps *b* and *c* for each remaining word in the column.
e. Repeat the column until children read all the words in order without making a mistake.

string
stand
stones
cash
pouch
smart
likes

Lesson 126

Stories for Lessons 112–170

In this lesson range, the program introduces longer serial stories. The longest series runs for fifteen lessons. The stories average 315 words.

Some of the stories involve plays on words. Some children are able to read the stories but fail to catch the significance of things that happen. For example, when Ott tries to make a *hot dog* appear, he gets a *hot log* instead. When such situations occur, *model the reaction you want from the children.* "Oh, that silly Ott. He didn't want a hot log, did he? I sure wish he were a better genie."

Follow this procedure whenever the children fail to react to something that is meant to be amusing. *You react.* When you reread the story, you will find that the children will react in the way you did.

Individual checkouts for rate and accuracy continue. At lesson 170, the last lesson in the program, children who pass the checkout read at least ninety words per minute.

Story Format for Lessons 112–114

At lesson 112, a major change occurs in the procedures you use to direct story reading. Group reading is dropped and individual reading replaces it. Children have been reading individually for their checkouts on rate and accuracy since lesson 54. Individual children now read two or three sentences for each reading turn. Children who lose their place lose their turn.

TASK 10 First reading

a. Everybody, get ready to read the story. Touch the title of the story. Check. We're going to read this story two times. The second time, I'll ask questions.
b. I'm going to call on different children to read two or three sentences. Everybody, follow along. If you hear a mistake, raise your hand. Children who do not have their place lose their turn. Call on individual children to read two or three sentences. Do not ask comprehension questions.

To correct word-identification errors (**from**, for example)
1. That word is **from**. What word? *From.*
2. Go back to the beginning of the sentence and read the sentence again.

TASK 11 Second reading

a. Everybody, you're going to read the story again. This time, I'm going to ask questions. Touch the title of the story. Check.
b. Call on individual children to read two or three sentences. Ask the specified questions at the end of each underlined sentence.

Lesson 112

Story Format for Lessons 115—170

Beginning at lesson 115, the stories appear in traditional textbook print. The presentation format from lesson 116 is shown below.

TASK 11 Reading—decoding

a. Everybody, look at the story on page 101. Check. You're going to read this story today. But before you read the story, turn to page 102. Check.

b. Everybody, in the middle of the story there's a big red number 5 in a circle. Touch that number 5. Check. That 5 tells you that, if the group reads all the way to the 5 without making more than five errors, we can go on in the story.. But if the group makes more than five errors, you have to go back and read the first part again. You have to keep reading it until you can read it without making more than five errors. I'll count the errors. Now turn back to page 101. Check. I'll tell you about the big star later.

c. Everybody, touch the title of the story. Check.

d. I'm going to call on different children to read two or three sentences. Everybody, follow along. If you hear a mistake, raise your hand. Children who do not have their place lose their turn. Call on individual children to read two or three sentences. Do not ask comprehension questions.

To correct word-identification errors (**from**, for example)
1. That word is **from.** What word? *From.*
2. Go back to the beginning of the sentence and read the sentence again.
3. Tally all errors.

e. If the children make more than five errors: when they reach the 5, say, You made too many errors. Go back to the beginning of the story and we'll try again. Try to read more carefully this time. Call on individual children to read two or three sentences. Do not ask comprehension questions. Repeat step e until firm, and then go on to step *f.*

f. When the children read to the number 5 without making more than five errors: say,

---

<u>**don has Super fun**</u>[1]
Who gave don the dime?[2]
Where did he tape the dime?[3]
<u>Was he doing good things?</u>[4]
<u>did don mope after he became a super man?</u>[5]

don was hopping around the store in his cap and his cape. he was hitting the walls and making holes. he was having a lot of fun.

all at once he stopped. <u>he said, "I will go outside and show what a super man I am."</u>[6]

When don left the store, he didn't open the door. he ran into the door. <u>"Crash."</u>[7]

Some boys were standing outside the store. They said, "look at that funny man in a cap and a cape."

---

don said, "I am no funny man. I am ★ a super man."

<u>don ran to a car that was parked near the store.</u>[8]<u>he picked the car up and gave it a big heave.</u>[9] The car crashed into another car. ⑤

The boys yelled, "let's get out of here. That man is a nut."

"Come back," don shouted. "let me show you how super I am."

<u>but the boys did not come back. They ran as fast as they could go.</u>[10]

don said, "I think I will fly to the top of this store." <u>So he did</u>[11] Then he said, "I think I will dive down to the street." So he did. he took a dive. "Crash." <u>he made a big hole in the street.</u>[12]

<u>"This is a lot of fun," don said.</u>[13]
<u>To be continued</u>[14]

Good reading. I'll read the story from the beginning to the 5 and ask you some questions. Read the story, starting with the title. Stop at the end of each underlined sentence and ask the specified question. When you reach the 5, call on individual children to continue reading the story. Have each child read two or three sentences. Ask the specified questions at the end of each underlined sentence.

[1] What's Don going to do in this story? (Signal.) *Have super fun.*
[2] Everybody, say that question. (Signal.) *Who gave Don the dime?* What's the answer? (Signal.) *The woman.*
[3] What's the answer? (Signal.) *To his arm.*
[4] Say that question. (Signal.) *Was he doing good things?* What's the answer? (Signal.) *No.*

[5] What's the answer? (Signal.) *No.*
[6] What's he going to do? (Signal.) *Go outside and show what a super man he is.*
[7] What went crash? (Signal.) *The door.* Why? *The children respond.*
[8] What do you think he'll do to that car? *The children respond.* Let's find out.
[9] What did he do to the car? *The children respond.*
[10] Who ran? (Signal.) *The boys.* Why did they run? *The children respond.* I don't blame them. I'd run away, too.
[11] What did he do? (Signal.) *Fly to the top of the store.*
[12] How did the hole get in the street? *The children respond.*
[13] What did he say? (Signal.) *This is a lot of fun.*
[14] Will there be more Don stories? (Signal.) *Yes.*

Lesson 116

Five-Error Mark

Note the big red circled 5 in the story above. The 5 denotes the five-error mark. You tally each error as individual children read.

If the group makes no more than five errors by the time it reaches the five-error mark, you reread the story to the children (from the beginning to the five-error mark), stopping at the end of each underlined sentence to ask the specified comprehension questions.

If the group makes more than five errors, the children reread the first part until they make no more than five errors.

The children then take turns reading. They read two or three sentences each from the five-error mark to the end of the story. Do not tally errors for this part, but continue to ask the comprehension questions. Note that the children read the complete story only one time and you read to the 5 one time.

PRACTICE presenting the format to your partner, who makes errors. When you reach step *e,* decide whether you should reread the story from the beginning to the 5 and ask the specified comprehension questions or if you should direct your partner back to the beginning of the story.

How to Read the Story to the Children

Children are very reinforced by this activity. They should follow along with their finger or a marker as you read.

One of your major goals in reading the story to the children is to model inflection, appropriate responses to story content, *and* rate. Adjust your rate so that you read to them a little faster—but only a little faster—than you expect them to read on their individual checkouts. A good way to know if you're reading at an appropriate rate is to watch the children's fingers as they follow along. If their fingers are not in place, you're probably reading too fast. Never read to them as fast as you would if you were reading a story aloud during library time.

PRACTICE timing yourself on story 116 (on page 69 of this guide). Start with the title and read to the five-error mark. There are 151 words. You should read this section (without asking questions for this practice) in two minutes.

Rate-and-Accuracy Checkouts (Lessons 116—170)

Starting at story 116, every checkout story is marked with a star (in addition to the five-error mark). The children read to the star for their individual checkouts.

The "Rule" Stories (Lessons 156—170)

The culmination of work in Fast Cycle II is the series of stories that runs from lesson 156 through 170. These stories contain all the types of words that have been taught. The stories also involve all the comprehension skills that have been taught. The stories are about Jean, who dreams that she is in a strange land— the land of peevish pets. Before she can leave the land, she must learn sixteen rules that hold for this strange land. The rules are presented in the stories. They are to be firmed on the first reading of the story, before the teacher rereads to the five-error mark.

Shown below are a passage from story 156 and the comprehension questions that pertain to the passage.

And right in the middle of her dream was an old wizard[5]

"Ho. ho." the wizard said to her. "What is your name?"

"Jean." she answered.

"Well. Jean." he said. "I hope you have a fine time here in the land of peevish pets. But you must remember this rule: All little crumps are mean."[6]

"What are little crumps?" Jean asked.

"That doesn't matter." the wizard answered. "Just remember the rule: All little crumps are mean."[7]

Jean said. "I'll remember that rule: All crumps are mean."[8]

"No. no." the wizard said. "All little crumps are mean."

"I've got it." Jean said. "But what and when . . . ."

The wizard was gone. and Jean was all alone in the land of peevish pets.[9]

More to come

[5] Who did she meet in her dream? (Signal.) *An old wizard.* Yes, a wizard does magic.

[6] Everybody, say that rule with me. (Signal.) Teacher and children say: *All little crumps are mean.* Repeat until firm. All by yourselves. Get ready. (Signal.) The children repeat the rule until firm.

[7] Everybody, what's the rule? (Signal.) *All little crumps are mean.*

[8] What did Jean say about crumps? (Signal.) *All crumps are mean.* Is that right? (Signal.) *No.* What's the rule? (Signal.) *All little crumps are mean.* Right. All little crumps are mean.

[9] What happened to the wizard? *The children respond.* Was Jean alone? (Signal.) *Yes.* Next time we'll read more about the crumps.

Lesson 156

Critical Behaviors

The rules presented in each story are used in subsequent stories. Therefore, it is important to firm them when they first appear in the story.

The rule in story 156 is, "All little crumps are mean." Follow these procedures for firming this rule:

1. *(Lead)* Everybody, say that rule with me. Set a cadence or rhythm for presenting rules. The children will learn to say them faster with a cadence as a prompt. A good idea is to divide the rule into two parts. For example, All *little* crumps (pause pause) are mean.

2. *(Test)* Expect lower-performing children to require perhaps ten repetitions on rules before they are firm in saying them. *Give them the repetition the first time the rule appears.* If you firm the children when a rule is first presented, they will have few problems with rule application.

PRACTICE step 1—leading the students. Use the cadence specified.

Rule Review (Lessons 157–170)

The rule-review task is presented before each story. In lesson 157, the rule "All little crumps are mean" is reviewed. Each of the sixteen rules is reviewed several times.

Below is the rule-review format for lesson 161. It reviews three rules.

```
TASK 5  Rule review

a. Everybody, you have  arned rules in the
   earlier Jean stories.
b. You learned a rule a         ' dusty path.
   Say that rule. Get rea     (Signal.) Every
   dusty path leads to the lake. Repeat until
   firm.
c. You learned a rule about every rocky path.
   Say that rule. Get ready. (Signal.) Every
   rocky path leads to the mountain. Repeat
   until firm.
d. You learned a rule about red food. Say that
   rule. Get ready. (Signal.) Red food is good
   to eat. Repeat until firm.
e. If the children missed any rules, repeat
   steps b through d.
```

Lesson 161

The rules in the land of peevish pets present to the children reinforcing tasks that are quite similar to tasks they will later encounter in textbooks:

- The children learn a system of information, not merely a single fact or isolated bits of information.

- They apply the information from story to story and from situation to situation. What is learned now is applied later to other situations in the system.

- The only difference between the rules in this series of stories and the rules that children learn in science and social studies is that the rules from the land of peevish pets are embedded in a story. Although names such as "crumps" are nonsense words, the process of learning the meaning of these words is no different from that involved with any unfamiliar word.

Take-Homes for Lessons 112–170

In this lesson range, a new track—Deductions—is introduced (lessons 126-170).

In the Story Items track, story-items review questions are introduced. They begin in lesson 127 and continue through lesson 157. The story-review items refer to stories that were read earlier. The goal of the exercises is to prompt the children to become facile in remembering information from day to day.

In the Reading-Comprehension track, nonfiction factual passages are introduced in lesson 151. These passages give the children practice in reading material that is designed to teach them something new. This skill is particularly important in reading textbooks.

Picture Deductions

Picture-deduction exercises appear in lessons 126 through 157. The format that introduces the exercise in lesson 126 and the related take-home activity are shown below.

> **TASK 7 Picture deductions**
>
> **a.** Pass out Take-Home 126 to each child.
> **b.** Hold up side 2 of your take-home and touch the sentence in the box in the deductions exercise.
> **c.** Everybody, touch this sentence on your take-home. Check children's responses.
> **d.** Call on a child. Read the sentence in the box. *All the big horses are tired.*
> **e.** Everybody, say that rule. (Signal.) *All the big horses are tired.* Repeat until firm.
> **f.** You know that some of the horses in the picture are tired. What kind of horses are those? (Signal.) *All the big horses.* Everybody, touch a horse you know is tired. Check.
> **g.** You don't know about the horses that are not big. Everybody, touch a horse you don't know about. Check.
> **h.** Call on a child. Read the instructions below the box. *Circle every horse that is tired.*
> **i.** Everybody, what are you going to do? (Signal.) *Circle every horse that is tired.* Yes, circle every horse that you know is tired.
> **j.** Do it. Check.

Lesson 126

All the big horses are tired.

Circle every horse that is tired.

Take-Home 126

Critical Behavior

In step *e*, the children are firmed on saying the rule "All the big horses are tired." Children who are low in language skills may require quite a few repetitions.

Corrections

In steps *f* and *g*, correct any mistakes this way:

1. What's the rule? The children respond: *All the big horses are tired.* Yes, *all the big horses are tired.*
2. Point to a horse. Everybody, is this horse big?... So do you know if this horse is tired?

Note: Children may respond to little horses in the following way:

> Teacher: **Is this horse big?**
> Children: *No.*
> Teacher: **So is this horse tired?**
> Children: *I don't know.* (Accept this response.)
> Teacher: **Good thinking. The rule only tells about the big horses.**

Track Development

The picture-deduction items are teacher directed in lessons 126 and 127. After lesson 127, the children work picture-deduction items independently. The rules that are presented through lesson 150 are of the following forms:

> All ____ are ____.
> (*All the big dogs are sleepy.*)
>
> Every ____ is ____.
> (*Every white box is made of wood.*)
>
> If ____, then ____.
> (*If a horse is running, it is old.*)
> (*If a cup has spots, it is hot.*)

At lesson 151, a more complex rule is introduced:

> Every ____ with a ____ will ____.
> (*Every man with a hat will go fishing.*)

If the children have trouble with this item, follow the firming procedure below:

1. Have the children read the rule aloud and then say it without reading it.
2. Point to each man and ask: **Is this a man *with a hat*?** Stress **with a hat**.
3. Then ask: **So will this man go fishing?**

If the children are unable to answer the first question, break the question into two parts:

1. Is this a man?... Does he have a hat?
2. Then ask: So will this man go fishing?

Written Deductions

In lesson 147, written deductions are introduced. They continue through the end of the program. Written deductions are similar to picture deductions except that they require the children to work from a written description of the examples, not from pictures.

Written Deductions Type 1

The Written Deductions Type 1 track begins in lesson 147 and continues through lesson 170. Below are the teacher presentation and the take-home activity for the written-deductions item from lesson 148.

TASK 8 Written deductions

a. Pass out Take-Home 148 to each child.
b. Hold up side 2 of your take-home and touch the sentence, "Every dog pants," in the deductions exercise.
c. Everybody, touch this sentence on your take-home. Check.
d. I'm going to call on different children to read a sentence. Everybody, follow along.
   1. Call on a child. Read the sentence in the box. *Every dog pants.* Everybody, what do you know about every dog? (Signal.) *It pants.* Yes, it pants.
   2. Call on a child. Read the sentence next to the box. *Rob is a dog.* Everybody, what do you know about Rob? (Signal.) *He is a dog.* And what do you know about every dog? (Signal.) *It pants.*
   3. Call on a child. Read the sentence under the box. *What does Rob do?* Everybody, listen. Every dog pants. Rob is a dog. So, what does he do? (Signal.) *He pants.* Yes, he pants.
e. Let's do that problem again. Repeat the sentence reading and questions in step *d.*
f. Everybody, write the answer in the blank. Check.

Lesson 148

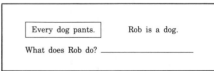

Every dog pants.   Rob is a dog.

What does Rob do? _____

Take-Home 148

Critical Behavior

When you present the format to the children, make sure that you firm them on step *d.* For some of the children, this may be the first time they have heard a conclusion of this type. Make sure they hear it frequently enough to become familiar with it.

PRACTICE steps *b* through *f* in the format from lesson 148. Also practice it with these rules:

All children go to school.
Juan and Linda are children.
What do Juan and Linda do?

Every house has windows.
I made a house.
What do you know about the house I made?

Correction

If the children make mistakes, ask them a "What do you know about . . .?" question for each sentence in the task. For example,

Every glip is red.
Tom is a glip.
What do you know about Tom?

1. Ask: What do you know about every glip? The children respond: *It's red.*
2. Ask: What do you know about Tom? The children respond: *He's a glip.*
3. Ask: So what else do you know about Tom? The children respond: *He's red.*

PRACTICE the above correction. Then practice the corrections with these rules:

Every car has doors.
Sid has a car.
What does Sid's car have?

Written Deductions Type 2

The Written Deductions Type 2 track begins in lesson 158 and continues through lesson 170. The track contains one format. Below are the teacher presentation and the children's take-home activity from lesson 158.

The teacher takes the children through the steps in the deduction. In step 8, the teacher instructs the children to write the names of everyone who has a house with bugs.

TASK 7   Written deductions

a. Pass out Take-Home 158 to each child.
b. Hold up side 1 of your take-home and touch the sentence above the box in the deductions exercise.
c. Everybody, touch this sentence on your take-home. Check.
d. I'm going to call on different children to read a sentence. Everybody, follow along.
  1. Call on a child. Read the sentence above the box. *Find out where the bugs are.* Everybody, what do you have to find out? (Signal.) *Where the bugs are.*
  2. Call on a child. Read the sentence in the box. *Here is the rule: Every white house has bugs.* Everybody, what's the rule? (Signal.) *Every white house has bugs.* You need that rule to find out where the bugs are.
  3. Call on a child. Read the first sentence below the box. *Kim's house is brown.* Everybody, is Kim's house white? (Signal.) *No.* And where are the bugs? (Signal.) *In every white house.* So we don't know if Kim's house has bugs.
  4. Call on a child. Read the next sentence. *Spot's house is white.* Everybody, is Spot's house white? (Signal.) *Yes.* And where are the bugs? (Signal.) *In every white house.* So does Spot's house have bugs? (Signal.) *Yes.* Yes, Spot's house has bugs.
  5. Call on a child. Read the next sentence. *Ott's house is white.* Everybody, is Ott's house white? *Yes.* And where are the bugs? (Signal.) *In every white house.* So does Ott's house have bugs? (Signal.) *Yes.* Yes, Ott's house has bugs.
  6. Call on a child. Read the next sentence. *Tim's house is red.* Everybody, is Tim's house white? (Signal.) *No.* And where are the bugs? (Signal.) *In every white house.* So we don't know if Tim's house has bugs.
  7. Call on a child. Read the next sentence. *Mom's house is black.* Everybody, is Mom's house white? (Signal.) *No.* And where are the bugs? (Signal.) *In every white house.* So we don't know if Mom's house has bugs.
  8. Call on a child. Read the last sentence. *Who has a house with bugs?* Everybody, what do you have to tell? (Signal.) *Who has a house with bugs.* Write in the blanks the names of everyone who has a house with bugs. Check.

Lesson 158

Find out where the bugs are.

| Here is the rule: Every white house has bugs. |

  Kim's house is brown.
  Spot's house is white.
  Ott's house is white.
  Tim's house is red.
  Mom's house is black.

Who has a house with bugs? _____ _____

Take-Home 158

Correction for Incorrect Names in Step 8

1. Have the children say the rule about where the bugs are.
2. Have them read each sentence below the box and make a circle after it if there are bugs in the house.
3. After the children have made a circle after every appropriate sentence, tell them: **Look at each sentence with a circle after it and find the name of the person who owns that house. Then write the name of that person on a line in the item.**

If the children are firmed on the procedures during lessons 158 through 160, they probably will have no trouble working the remaining items on the track without supervision and without making mistakes.

Story-Items Review

The Story-Items Review track begins in lesson 127 and continues through lesson 157. The track contains one format.

The story-items-review exercise in lesson 127 refers to stories that were read in lessons 122 and 125.

TASK 7   Children read and do story-items review

a. Pass out Take-Home 127 to each child.
b. Hold up side 1 of your take-home and point to the row of stars below story item 7.
c. Everybody, touch this row of stars on your take-home. Check children's responses.
d. The items below the stars are about an old story. You didn't read that story today.
e. Everybody, get ready to read item 1. First word. Check children's responses. Get ready. Clap for each word as the children read: *Did Sid tap the oak tree or tape the oak tree?*
f. What's the answer to item 1? (Signal.) *Tap the oak tree.* Yes, **tap the oak tree.**
g. Everybody, write the answer in the blank. Check children's responses.
h. Read item 2 to yourself and raise your hand when you know the answer.
i. When all the hands are raised, say, Everybody, what's the answer to item 2? (Signal.) *The boss.*
j. Everybody, write the answer in the blank. Check children's responses.
k. Everybody, you'll do the other item later.

Lesson 127

---

1. Did Sid tap the oak tree or tape the oak tree?

_____ the oak tree

2. Who told Sid, "I will teach you to read"?

_____

3. Did Sid become good at reading? _____

Take-Home 127

Corrections

- If the children have trouble answering the question at step *f*, tell them the answer and structure the other items. (Have the children read the question and then answer it.)

- If you check the children's independent work and find that they cannot remember the answers to the review items, you can refer them to the appropriate storybook page, which you will find noted in the Teacher's Take-Home Book.

Story Items

In lesson 145 (the lesson following the end of the Following Instructions track), the story-items activities incorporate directions of the form that had been in the following-instructions activities. The teacher presentation and the story items from lesson 145 are shown here.

Practice the format before presenting it to the children. The format appears in two lessons—145 and 146. It is a good idea to monitor the children as they work the items. If they make mistakes, refer them to the instructions that appear in the box for the item they are working. Tell them to read the instructions and then work the item again.

A major objective of the story items is to give the children a great deal of practice in following written directions. The more facile they become in following them, the less trouble they will have reading for new information in later grades.

TASK 9 Following instructions

a. Pass out Take-Home 145 to each child.
b. Hold up side 1 of your take-home and point to the story-items exercise.
c. Everybody, touch item 1. Check children's responses.
d. Everybody, touch the instructions in the box above item 1. Check children's responses. Those instructions tell you how to work item 1. Call on a child. Read the instructions in the box. *Make a line under the answer.*
e. Everybody, what are you going to do to answer item 1? (Signal.) *Make a line under the answer.*
f. Everybody, touch the instructions in the box above item 2. Check children's responses. Those instructions tell you how to work items 2 and 3. Call on a child. Read the instructions in the box. *Fill in the blanks.*
g. Everybody, are you going to circle the answers? (Signal.) *No.* Are you going to make a line under the answers? (Signal.) *No.*
h. What are you going to do to work items 2 and 3? (Signal.) *Fill in the blanks.*
i. Everybody, touch the instructions in the box above item 4. Check children's responses. Those instructions tell you how to work item 4. Call on a child. Read the instructions in the box. *Circle the answer.*
j. Everybody, are you going to make a line under the answer? (Signal.) *No.* Are you going to fill in the blanks? (Signal). *No.*
k. What are you going to do to work item 4? (Signal.) *Circle the answer.*
l. Everybody, touch the instructions in the box above item 5. Check children's responses. Those instructions tell you how to work items 5 and 6. Call on a child. Read the instructions in the box. *Fill in the blanks.*
m. Everybody, are you going to make a line under the answers? (Signal.) *No.* Are you going to circle the answers? (Signal.) *No.*
n. What are you going to do to work items 5 and 6? (Signal.) *Fill in the blanks.*
o. You'll work the items later. Remember to follow the instructions that go with each item.

Lesson 145

Make a line under the answer.

1. Carla was _____ from Ott's school book.
   reading   sitting   laughing

Fill in the blanks.

2. Carla said, "Ib, bub, ib, bub, ib, bub, bibby. Bome, _____ ,

_____ . I want to go _____ , _____ ,

_____ ."

3. Who said, "That is too much to remember"? _____

Circle the answer.

4. Who sent Carla home?
   an old genie   Carla   Ott

Fill in the blanks.

5. Did Ott go to Carla's home? _____

6. Who said, "I better call for help"? _____

Take-Home 145

Reading Comprehension: Factual Information Passages

In lesson 151, the first *factual information* reading-comprehension selection is introduced. These factual information passages continue through lesson 170.

In many of the reading-comprehension passages from lessons 151 to 170, new science and social-science information is introduced. Children apply some facts to passages in later lessons. In lesson 163, for example, the children learn that all living things grow. The rule is reviewed in lesson 164. In that selection the children are also taught more information about living things.

The children apply the skills they have learned in deductions exercises to these factual information passages. Below are the teacher's directions and the comprehension selection for lesson 151.

TASK 7 Reading comprehension

a. Pass out Take-Home 151 to each child.
b. Everybody, turn to side 2 of your take-home. Check.
c. Point to the story on side 2 of your take-home. Everybody, find this story on your take-home. Check.
d. Today you're going to read a passage that tells about weeds.
e. Everybody, touch the picture of the first plant. Check. That's a weed.
f. Everybody, touch the picture of the next plant. Check. That's a weed.
g. Everybody, touch the picture of the next plant. Check. That's a rose. What is it? (Signal.) *A rose.*
h. I'll read the passage. Everybody, follow along. Read the passage to the children. Check that they are following along as you read.
i. When you do your independent work, read the passage to yourself. Then answer the questions.

Lesson 151

A weed is a plant that people don't want. In some parts of the world, a rose is called a weed. We think a rose is a pretty flower. But it is a weed when it grows where nobody wants it. And we like some plants that grow like weeds in other parts of the world.

Fill in the blanks.

1. A weed is a _____ that people don't _____ .
2. Could a pretty flower be a weed? _____
3. Could a big plant be a weed? _____
4. A plant that you buy is not a _____ .
5. Could a rose be a weed? _____

Take-Home 151

Critical Behaviors

Check to see that the children touch the correct pictures in steps *e* through *g*. For many children, this selection is the first science information they have read.

Read the passage to the children as they follow along. (Read at the same rate as you do when you read the stories. See page 70.) Starting at lesson 161 you do not read the passage. The children do all the activities independently during their seatwork. Attend carefully to their take-home answers. Take the time to correct and firm.

Corrections

The most frequent type of mistake the children make is that of not remembering the information in the story. The children may either write down nonsense answers or go on to something else. Correct in the following way:

1. Have the children read the item aloud.
2. Say: **What's the answer?**
3. If they are unable to answer the question, say: **That's a hard question, but you can find the answer if you read the story again.**

Appendix

Sample Lessons

Lessons 4 and 81 and their corresponding Storybook
and Take-Home materials are reproduced here in
their entirety so that you can practice the skills
discussed in this guide before presenting Reading
Mastery to your students.

Lesson 4

PRONUNCIATION

TASK 1 Children say the sounds

a. You're going to say some sounds. When I hold up my finger, say, (pause) ēēē. Get ready. Hold up one finger. ēēē.
b. Next sound. Say (pause) rrr. Get ready. Hold up one finger. rrr.
c. Next sound. Say (pause) nnn. Get ready. Hold up one finger. nnn.
d. Repeat c for sounds ēēē, rrr, and nnn.
e. Call on different children to do a, b, or c.
f. Good saying the sounds.

SOUNDS

TASK 2 Sounds firm-up

a. Point to the column of sounds. See if you can say all these sounds without making a mistake. Touch the first ball of the arrow for **s**. (Pause one second.) Get ready. Move quickly to the second ball. Hold. sss.
   Yes, **sss.**
b. Touch the first ball of the arrow for **s.** (Pause one second.) Get ready. Move quickly to the second ball. Hold. sss.
   Yes, **sss.**
c. Repeat b for each remaining sound in the column.
d. Repeat the column until all children are firm on all sounds.
e. Call on different children to say all the sounds in the column.
f. Good. You said all the sounds in the column.

SAY THE SOUNDS—SAY IT FAST

TASK 3 Children say a word or sound slowly, then say it fast

a. I'm going to say some words and some sounds. First you're going to say them slowly. Then you're going to say them fast.
b. Listen. Hold up a finger for each sound. Say (pause) **rrraaat. Get ready.** Hold up a finger for each sound. *Rrraaat.*
   Again. Get ready. Hold up a finger for each sound. *Rrraaat.*
   Say it fast. (Signal.) *Rat.* Yes, **rat.**
c. Listen. Hold up one finger. Say (pause) īīī. Get ready. Hold up one finger. *īīī.*
   Again. Get ready. Hold up one finger. *īīī.*
   Say it fast. (Signal.) *ī.*
   Yes, **ī.**
d. Listen. Hold up a finger for each sound. Say (pause) **zzzooooo. Get ready.** Hold up a finger for each sound. *Zzzooooo.*
   Again. Get ready. Hold up a finger for each sound. *Zzzooooo.*
   Say it fast. (Signal.) *Zoo.*
   Yes, **zoo.**
e. Repeat b through d until firm.
f. Call on different children to do b, c, or d.

4

Do not show the picture until step *g*, task 4.

SAY IT FAST

TASK 4   Children say it fast, then see a picture

a. Do not show the picture until step *g*.

b. Say it fast and I'll show you a picture.

c. Listen. **Piiicnic.** (Pause.) Say it fast! (Signal.) *Picnic.*
   What word? (Signal.) *Picnic.*

d. Yes, what is the picture going to show? (Signal.) *Picnic.* **Yes, picnic.**

e. In the picture you will see a family in the park having a . . . . (Pause.) **Piiicnic.** (Pause.) Say it fast! (Signal.) *Picnic.*

f. Repeat *e* until firm.

g. Here's the picture.

4

SOUNDS—SAY IT FAST

TASK 5 Children say a sound slowly, then say it fast

a. Touch the first ball of the arrow for **s.** First you're going to say it slowly. Then you're going to say it fast. Say it slowly. Get ready. Move quickly under each sound. Hold under each sound for one second. *sssss.*
Return to the first ball for **s.** Say it fast. Slash. *s.* Yes, *s.*
b. Repeat *a* until firm.
c. Touch the first ball of the arrow for **a.** Say it slowly. Get ready. Move quickly to the second ball. Hold. *aaa.*
Return to the first ball for **a.** Say it fast. Slash. *a.* Yes, *a.*
d. Repeat *c* until firm.
e. Call on different children to do *a* or *c.*

SOUNDS

TASK 6 Introducing the new sound ēēē as in ēat

a. Touch the first ball of the arrow. Here's a new sound. My turn to say it. Get ready. Move quickly to the second ball. Hold. *ēēē.*
b. Touch the first ball of the arrow. My turn again. Get ready. Move quickly to the second ball. Hold. *ēēē.*
c. Touch the first ball of the arrow. My turn again. Get ready. Move quickly to the second ball. Hold. *ēēē.*
d. Touch the first ball of the arrow. Your turn. Get ready. Move quickly to the second ball. Hold. *ēēē.* Yes, *ēēē.*
e. Touch the first ball of the arrow. Again. Get ready. Move quickly to the second ball. Hold. *ēēē.* Yes, *ēēē.*
f. Repeat *e* until firm.
g. Call on different children to do *d.*
h. Good saying *ēēē.*

SOUND OUT

TASK 7 Children say the sounds without stopping

a. Touch the first ball of the arrow for **sa.** My turn. I'll show you how to say these sounds without stopping between the sounds. Move under each sound. Hold. Say *sssaaa.*
b. Return to the first ball of the arrow for **sa.** Your turn. Say the sounds as I touch under them. Don't stop between the sounds. Get ready. Move under each sound. Hold. *Sssaaa.*
Return to the first ball of the arrow. Again. Get ready. Move under each sound. Hold. *Sssaaa.*
Good saying *sssaaa.*
c. Touch the first ball of the arrow for **ma.** My turn. I'll show you how to say these sounds without stopping between the sounds. Move under each sound. Hold. Say *mmmaaa.*
d. Return to the first ball of the arrow for **ma.** Your turn. Say the sounds as I touch under them. Don't stop between the sounds. Get ready. Move under each sound. Hold. *Mmmaaa.*
Return to the first ball of the arrow. Again. Get ready. Move under each sound. Hold. *Mmmaaa.*
Good saying *mmmaaa.*
e. Call on different children to do *b* or *d.*

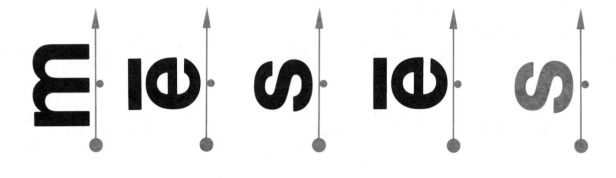

4

SOUNDS

TASK 8 Sounds firm-up

a. Point to **ē**. Remember, this new sound is (pause) **ēēē**.

b. Point to the column of sounds. See if you can say these sounds without making a mistake. Touch the first ball of the arrow for **m**. (Pause one second.) Get ready. Move quickly to the second ball. Hold. *mmm*. **Yes, mmm.**

c. Touch the first ball of the arrow for **ē**. (Pause one second.) Get ready. Move quickly to the second ball. Hold. *ēēē*. **Yes, ēēē.**

d. Repeat c for each remaining sound in the column.

e. Repeat the column until all children are firm on all sounds.

f. Call on different children to say all the sounds in the column.

g. **Good. You said all the sounds in the column.**

82   Fast Cycle Teacher's Guide

4

SAY IT FAST—RHYMING
This is an oral task.

TASK 9 Children say word parts slowly, then say them fast

a. Let's do the hard Say It Fast. Listen. Hold up one finger. First you'll say (pause) **mmm**. Hold up two fingers. (pause) **aaat**. Listen again. Hold up one finger. First you'll say (pause) **mmm**. Hold up two fingers. (pause) **aaat**.

b. Say it slowly. Get ready. Hold up one finger. *mmm*.
Hold up two fingers. *Mmmaaat*.

c. Again. Get ready. Hold up one finger. *mmm*.
Hold up two fingers. *Mmmaaat*. Say it fast. (Signal.) *Mat*. Yes, **mat.**

d. Repeat a through c until firm.

e. Here's a new word. Listen. Hold up one finger. First you'll say (pause) **fff**. Hold up two fingers. (pause) **uuunnn**. Listen again. Hold up one finger. First you'll say (pause) **fff**. Hold up two fingers. (pause) **uuunnn**.

f. Say it slowly. Get ready. Hold up one finger. *fff*.
Hold up two fingers. *Ffuuunnn*.

g. Again. Get ready. Hold up one finger. *fff*.
Hold up two fingers. *Ffuuunnn*. Say it fast. (Signal.) *Fun*. Yes, **fun.**

h. Repeat e through g until firm.

i. Here's a new word. Listen. Hold up one finger. First you'll say (pause) **zzz**. Hold up two fingers. Then you'll say (pause) **ooooo**. Listen again. First you'll say (pause) **zzz**. Hold up two fingers. Then you'll say (pause) **ooooo**. Hold up one finger. *zzz*.
Hold up two fingers. *Zzzooooooo*.

k. Again. Get ready. Hold up one finger. *zzz*.
Hold up two fingers. *Zzzooooooo*. Say it fast. (Signal.) *Zoo*. Yes, **zoo.**

l. Repeat i through k until firm.

m. Call on different children to do a–c, e–g, or i–k.

Take-Home 4

SAY IT FAST

TASK 10 Children say the word fast

a. The word you will say tells what you're going to see on your take-home. Listen. **Juuummmps.** (Pause.) Say it fast! (Signal.) *Jumps.*

b. Get ready to do it again. Listen. **Juuummmps.** (Pause.) Say it fast! (Signal.) *Jumps.*

c. Yes, the picture on your take-home will show an animal that really . . . . . (Signal.) *Jumps.* Yes, **jumps.**

TASK 11 Individual test

a. Call on each child. [Child's name], listen. **Juuummmps.** (Pause.) Say it fast! (Signal.) *Jumps.*

b. Give a take-home to each child after he or she says the word fast.

SOUND OUT

TASK 12 Children move their finger under s or ē and say it

a. Everybody, finger on the first ball of the first arrow. Check children's responses. When I clap, quickly move your finger under the sound and say it. (Pause.) Get ready. Clap. Children move their finger under **s** and say sss. Yes, sss.

b. Again. Finger on the first ball of the first arrow. Check children's responses. Get ready. Clap. Children move their finger under **s** and say sss. Yes, sss.

c. Repeat *b* until firm.

d. Everybody, finger on the first ball of the next arrow. Check children's responses. When I clap, quickly move your finger under the sound and say it. (Pause.) Get ready. Clap. Children move their finger under **ē** and say ēēē. Yes, ēēē.

e. Again. Finger on the first ball of the arrow. Check children's responses. Get ready. Clap. Children move their finger under **ē** and say ēēē. Yes, ēēē.

f. Repeat *e* until firm.

TASK 13 Individual test

a. Call on a child. Show the child which ball to touch. Get ready. Clap. *Child moves finger under the sound and says it.*

b. Call on different children to do *a.*

c. Good. You really know how to move your finger under the sound and say it.

4

TASK 14 Children touch under the sounds

a. Hold up side 1 of your take-home. Touch the first ball of the arrow for **am.** Put your finger on the first ball of this arrow. Check. Put down your take-home.

b. I'm going to say the sounds without stopping. You're going to touch under the sounds as I say them. Quickly move your finger under each sound when I say it. I'll say the sounds you touch. Get ready. **aaammm.** Hold each sound for two seconds. Check that the children are moving their finger under each sound as you say it.

c. Again. Finger on the first ball of the arrow. Check children's responses. Get ready. **Aaammm.** Hold each sound for two seconds. Check that the children are moving their finger under each sound as you say it.

d. Repeat **c** until firm.

TASK 15 Individual test

a. Call on a child. Finger on the first ball of the arrow. Check the child's response. Quickly move your finger under each sound as I say it. Get ready. **Aaammm.** Hold each sound for two seconds.

b. Call on different children to do **a.**

c. Good moving your finger under each sound.

SOUND WRITING
The children will need pencils.

TASK 16 Children write ē

a. Point to the dotted **ē.** Everybody, what sound are you going to write? (Signal.) *ēēē.*

b. Get ready to show me the ball you're going to start with. (Pause.) Get ready. (Signal.) *The children touch the big ball.* Put your pencil on the big ball and write **ēēē.** Check children's responses.

c. Point to the top row of dotted **ē's.** Everybody, now you're going to write **ēēē** in this row until I tell you to stop.

d. After a minute say: Stop. You will finish writing **ēēē** later.

SUMMARY OF INDEPENDENT ACTIVITY

TASK 17 Introduction to independent activity

a. Hold up Take-Home 4.

b. Everybody, you're going to finish this take-home on your own. Tell the children when they will work the remaining items. Let's go over the things you're going to do.

TASK 18 Sound writing

Point to the sound-writing exercise on side 1. You're going to finish writing **ēēē.** What are you going to write? (Signal.) *ēēē.*

TASK 19 Cross-out game

a. Point to the Cross-out Game on side 2. Here's the Cross-out Game.

b. Point to the box with the cross-out **a.** Everybody, what sound are you going to cross out? (Signal.) *aaa.*

TASK 20 Picture completion

Point to the picture-completion exercise. After you do the Cross-out Game, follow the dots and finish this picture. Then you can color it.

END OF LESSON 4

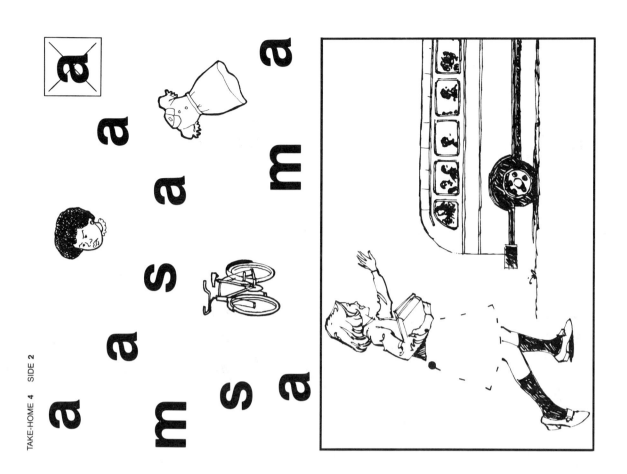

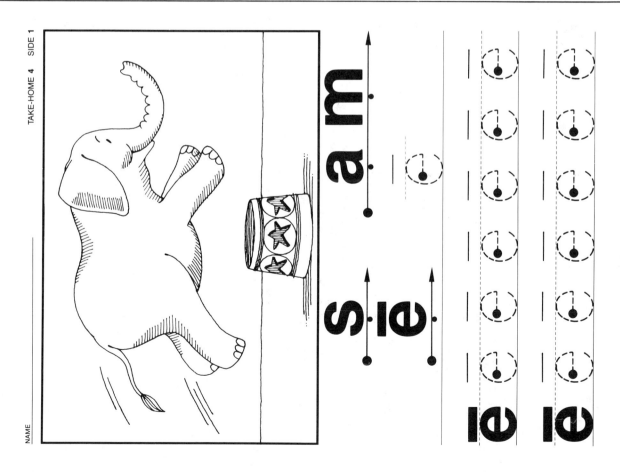

ā   e   a

wh   th   ē

y   sh   ch

p   h   g

LESSON 81

SOUNDS

TASK 1 Sounds firm-up

a. Point to the sounds.
   Tell me these sounds.

b. **When I touch it, you say it.**
   Keep on saying it as long as I touch it.

c. Point to each sound. **Get ready.**
   Touch the sound. *The children say the sound.* Lift your finger.

To correct

1. Immediately say the correct sound as you continue to touch it. Lift your finger.

2. **Say it with me.** Touch sound and say it with children. Lift your finger.

3. **Again.** Repeat until firm.

4. **All by yourselves. Get ready.** Touch the sound. *The children say the sound.*

d. Repeat problem sounds until the children can correctly identify all sounds in order.

Individual test

Call on several children to identify one or more sounds.

READING VOCABULARY

Do not touch small letters.

Get ready to read all the words on this page without making a mistake.

To correct

Have the children sound out and tell what word.

where

TASK 2   Sound out first

a. Touch the ball for **where.** Sound it out. Get ready. Quickly touch under **wh, e, r** as the children say *whwhwheeerr.*

b. What word? (Signal.) *Where.* Yes, **where.**

c. Repeat task until firm.

there

TASK 3   Sound out first

a. Touch the ball for **there.** Sound it out. Get ready. Quickly touch under **th, e, r** as the children say *thththeeerrr.*

b. What word? (Signal.) *There.* Yes, **there.**

c. Repeat task until firm.

ar

TASK 4   ar

a. Point to **ar.** When these letters are together, they usually say (pause) **are.** What do these letters say? (Signal.) *Are.* Yes, **are.**

b. Repeat *a* until firm.

arf

TASK 5   ar word

a. Point to **ar** in **arf.** What do these letters say? (Signal.) *Are.* Yes, **are.**

b. Touch the ball for **arf.** Read this word the fast way. Get ready. (Signal.) *Arf.* Yes, **arf.**

c. Repeat *a* and *b* for **barking.**

barking

shark

TASK 6   Read ar word the fast way

a. Touch the ball for **shark.** Read this word the fast way. (Pause two seconds.) Get ready. (Signal.) *Shark.* Yes, **shark.**

b. Point to **ar** in **shark.** Everybody, what do these letters say? (Signal.) *Are.* Yes, **are.**

c. Touch the ball for **shark.** Sound it out. Get ready. Quickly touch under **sh, ar, k** as the children say *shshshark.*

d. What word? (Signal.) *Shark.* Yes, **shark.**

e. Repeat *c* and *d* until firm.

other

TASK 7   Sound out first

a. Touch the ball for **other.** Sound it out. Get ready. Quickly touch under **o, th, er** as the children say *ooooththerrr.*

b. What word? (Signal.) *Other.* Yes, **other.**

c. Repeat task until firm.

Repeat any troublesome words.

Individual test

Call on different children. Each child reads a different word.

Do not touch small letters.
Get ready to read all the words on this page without making a mistake.

To correct
Have the children sound out and tell what word.

līked

yelled

awāy

swimming

help

swam

helped

after

TASK 9   Read the fast way first

a. Touch the ball for **help**. Read this word the fast way. (Pause two seconds.) Get ready. (Signal.) *Help.* Yes, **help**. Return to the ball. Sound it out.

b. Get ready. Quickly touch under **h, e, l, p** as the children say *heeelllp*.

c. What word? (Signal.) *Help.* Yes, **help**.

d. Repeat *b* and *c* until firm.

e. Repeat the task for **helped, after, līked, yelled, awāy,** and **swimming**.

Repeat any troublesome words.

Individual test
Call on different children. Each child reads a different word.

TASK 8   Last part, first part

a. Cover **s**. Point to **wam**. Read this part of the word the fast way. (Pause two seconds.) Get ready. (Signal.) *Wam.* Yes, **wam**.

b. Uncover **s**. Point to **s**. First you say *sss*. Move your finger quickly under **wam**. Then you say (pause) **wam**.

c. Touch the ball for **swam**. Get ready. Move to **s**, then quickly along the arrow. *Sssswam*.

d. Say it fast. (Signal.) *Swam.* Yes, what word? (Signal.) *Swam.* Yes, **swam**. Good reading.

e. Repeat *c* and *d* until firm.

81

Do not touch small letters.
Get ready to read all the words on this page without making a mistake.

To correct
Have the children sound out and tell what word.

TASK 10 Read the fast way

a. Read these words the fast way.
b. Touch the ball for **another.**
(Pause two seconds.) Get ready. (Signal.) *Another.* Yes, **another.**
c. Repeat *b* for **why, when,** and **funny.**

another

whȳ

when

funny

book

TASK 11 Listen, sound out

a. Point to **book.** I'll tell you this word. (Pause.) **Book.** What word? (Signal.) *Book.* Yes, **book.**
b. Touch the ball for **book.** Sound it out. Get ready. Quickly touch under **b, oo, k** as the children say *boook.*

To correct
If the children do not say the sounds you point to
1. Say: You've got to say the sounds I point to.
2. Repeat *b* until firm.

c. What word? (Signal.) *Book.* Yes, **book.**
d. Repeat *b* and *c* until firm.

took

TASK 12 Read the fast way first

a. Touch the ball for **took.** Read this word the fast way. (Pause two seconds.) Get ready. (Signal.) *Took.* Yes, **took.**
b. Return to the ball. Sound it out. Get ready. Quickly touch under **t, oo, k** as the children say *toook.*
c. What word? (Signal.) *Took.* Yes, **took.**
d. Repeat *b* and *c* until firm.

TASK 13 Read the fast way

a. Read these words the fast way.
b. Touch the ball for **looked.**
(Pause two seconds.) Get ready. (Signal.) *Looked.* Yes, **looked.**
c. Repeat *b* for **cooked.**

looked

cooked

Individual test
Call on individual children to read a column of words from this lesson. If the column contains only one or two words, direct the child to read additional words from an adjacent column. Praise children who read all words with no errors.

STORYBOOK

STORY 81

TASK 14 First reading—title and three sentences

a. Pass out Storybook 2.

b. Everybody, open your reader to page 1.

c. Everybody, touch the title. Check to see that the children are touching under the first word of the title.

d. I'll clap and you read each word in the title the fast way. Don't sound it out. Just tell me the word.

e. First word. Check children's responses. (Pause two seconds.) Get ready. Clap. The children read *Arf.*

f. Next word. Check to see that the children are touching under the next word. (Pause two seconds.) Get ready. Clap. The children read *the.*

g. Repeat f for the remaining word in the title.

h. Everybody, say the title.- (Signal.) *Arf the shark.* **Yes, Arf the shark.**

i. Everybody, get ready to read this story the fast way.

j. First word. Check children's responses. (Pause two seconds.) Get ready. Clap. *Arf.*

k. Next word. Check children's responses. (Pause two seconds.) Get ready. Clap. *Was.*

l. Repeat k for the remaining words in the first three sentences. Have the children reread the first three sentences until firm.

TASK 15 Remaining sentences

a. I'm going to call on different children to read a sentence. Everybody, follow along and point to the words. If you hear a mistake, raise your hand.

b. Call on a child. Read the next sentence.

To correct word-identification errors (**from**, for example)

1. That word is **from**. What word? *From.*

2. Go back to the beginning of the sentence and read the sentence again.

c. Call on a different child. Read the next sentence.

d. Repeat c for most of the remaining sentences in the story.

e. Occasionally have the group read a sentence. When the group is to read, say: Everybody, read the next sentence. (Pause two seconds.) Clap for each word in the sentence. Pause at least two seconds between claps.

NOTE: Underlined and numbered statements in the following copy of story 81 refer to questions you are to ask the children in task 16.

arf the shark¹

arf was a barking shark. arf was a little shark, but she had a big bark that made the other fish swim away.²

a shark swam up to arf and said, "you are a shark. let's play."

arf was happy. "arf, arf," she said.³ and the other shark swam far, far away. arf was not happy now.⁴

another shark swam up to arf. "you are a shark," he said. "let's play."

arf was happy. "arf, arf," she said. and the other shark swam far, far away. arf was not happy now.

then a big, big fish that liked to eat sharks swam up to the other sharks.⁵

"help, help," they yelled.⁶

but the big fish was swimming after them very fast. stop⁷

TASK 16 Second reading—sentences and questions

a. You're going to read the story again. This time I'm going to ask questions.

b. Starting with the first word of the title. Get ready. Check children's responses. Clap as the children read the title.

c. Call on a child. Read the first sentence.

To correct word-identification errors (**from**, for example)

1. That word is **from**. What word? *From.*
2. Go back to the beginning of the sentence and read the sentence again.

d. Call on a different child. Read the next sentence.

e. Repeat *d* for most of the remaining sentences in the story.

f. Occasionally have the group read a sentence.

g. After each underlined sentence has been read, present each comprehension question specified below to the entire group.

¹ What's this story about? (Signal.) *Arf the shark.*

² Who was Arf? (Signal.) *A little shark.*

³ What did Arf say? (Signal.) *Arf, arf.* Let's hear you say it like Arf said it. (Signal.) *Arf, arf.*

⁴ Why wasn't she happy? *The children respond.*

⁵ What did the big fish like to eat? (Signal.) *Sharks.* Let's see if the big fish eats any. ⁶ Why did the sharks yell? *The children respond.*

⁷ Is this the end of the story? (Signal.) *No.* Right. We stop now. We'll finish the story next time.

TASK 17 Picture comprehension

a. Look at the picture.

b. Ask these questions:

1. Show me the shark you think is Arf. *The children respond.*
2. What does it look like Arf is doing? *The children respond.*
3. What is that big fish doing? *The children respond.*
4. What would you do if you were Arf? Let the children comment for ten seconds. Then comment briefly.

TAKE-HOME 81

STORY ITEMS

TASK 18 Read the story items

a. Pass out Take-Home 81 to each child.
b. Hold up side 1 of your take-home and point to the story items exercise. **Everybody, you're going to read the items for the story you just read. You're going to circle the answers later.**
c. Touch the blank in item 1. **Here's where something is missing. When you get to this blank, say "blank."**
d. **Get ready to read item 1 the fast way. First word.** Check children's responses. Get ready. Clap. *Arf.*
e. **Next word.** Check children's responses. Get ready. Clap. *Was.*
f. Repeat e for the remaining words in item 1. . . . .
g. **Tell me the answer. Arf was a barking. . . .** (Signal.) *Shark.* **What word goes in the blank?** (Signal.) *Shark.* **The children are not to circle the answers now.**
h. Repeat *d* through *g* for item 2.
i. **You're going to do these items later. Remember to circle the right answer for each item.**

SENTENCE COPYING

TASK 19 Read sentence to copy

a. Point to the sentence **shē is in a car.**
b. **Here's the sentence you're going to write on the lines below. Everybody, touch this sentence on your take-home.** Check children's responses.
c. **Get ready to read the words in this sentence the fast way. First word.** Check children's responses. Get ready. Clap for each word as the children read: *She is in a car.*
d. **Have the children reread the sentence the fast way.**
e. **Point to the dotted words on the first line. Later, you're going to trace the dotted words in this sentence. Then you're going to write these words on the other lines.**

SOUND WRITING

TASK 20 Identify sounds to be written

a. Point to the sound-writing exercise. **Everybody, here are the sounds you're going to write today. I'll touch the sounds. You say them.**
b. **Touch each sound.** *The children respond.*
c. **Repeat** *b* until firm.
d. **You're going to write a sound on each bar. You'll write the sounds later.**

READING COMPREHENSION

The children will need pencils.

TASK 21 Read story, answer items

a. Hold up side 2 of your take-home and point to the word **reading. Everybody, touch this story on your take-home.** Check children's responses.
b. **Reading the fast way. First word.** Check children's responses. Get ready. Clap. *A.*
c. **Next word.** Check children's responses. Get ready. Clap. *Boy.*
d. Repeat *c* for the remaining words in the story.
e. Hold up your take-home. **Touch the blank in item 1. Everybody, here's where something is missing. When you get to this blank, say "blank."**
f. **Reading item 1 the fast way. First word.** Check children's responses. Get ready. Clap. *A.*
g. **Next word.** Check children's responses. Get ready. Clap. *Blank.*
h. Repeat *g* for the remaining words in item 1. Children read *ate cake.*
i. **Everybody, what word goes in the blank?** (Signal.) *Boy.*
j. Repeat *i* until firm.
k. **Look at the words under item 1 and get ready to touch the word that goes in the blank.** (Pause.) **Get ready.** (Signal.) Check children's responses.
l. **Circle the word boy.** Check children's responses.
m. Repeat *f* through *l* for item 2.

81

PICTURE COMPREHENSION

TASK 22 Write words for picture

Refer to sounds, not letter names, in missing words.

a. Hold up side 2 of your take-home and point to the first picture.
Look at this picture. Tell me what you see. Accept reasonable responses.

b. **Everybody, who looks old?** (Signal.) *The man.* Yes, this man is old.

c. **Everybody, what is the man holding?** (Signal.) *A rug.* Yes, he has a . . . . . (Signal.) *Rug.*

d. Repeat *b* and *c* until firm.

e. Point to the sound in the blank in item 1. **Something is missing. When you get to this, say "blank." What will you say?** (Signal.) *Blank.*

f. **Everybody, touch item 1 next to the picture.** Check children's responses.

g. **Get ready to read item 1 the fast way. First word.** Check children's responses. Get ready. Clap. *This.*
Next word. Check children's responses. Get ready. Clap. *Blank.*

i. Repeat *h* for the remaining words in item 1.

j. Repeat *g* through *i* until firm.

k. **What word goes in the blank?** (Signal.) *Man.*

l. **I'll say the sounds in the word man.** mmm (pause) aaa (pause) nnn. Again. mmm (pause) aaa (pause) nnn.

m. **Your turn. Say the sounds in man.** Get ready. Signal for each sound as the children say *mmm* (pause) *aaa* (pause) *nnn*.

n. Repeat *l* and *m* until firm.

o. **Look at the blank in item 1. The mmm is already written in the blank. So what sounds are you going to write next?** Signal for each sound as the children say *aaa* (pause) *nnn*. Repeat until firm.

p. **Everybody, write the missing sounds for man.** Check children's responses.

q. Repeat *g* through *p* for item 2.

r. **You'll do the items for the other picture later.**

SUMMARY OF INDEPENDENT ACTIVITY

TASK 23 Introduction to independent activity

a. Hold up side 1 of Take-Home 81.

b. **Everybody, you're going to finish this take-home on your own.** Tell the children when they will work the remaining items. Let's go over the things you're going to do.

TASK 24 Story items

Point to the story items exercise. **Remember to read the items and circle the answers that tell what happened in the story.**

TASK 25 Sentence copying

Point to the first line in the sentence-copying exercise. **Remember—you're going to trace the words in this sentence. Then you're going to write the sentence on the other lines.**

TASK 26 Sound writing

Point to the sound-writing exercise. **Remember to write a sound on each bar.**

TASK 27 Picture comprehension

a. Point to the second picture in the picture-comprehension exercise.
Everybody, you're going to look at this picture. Then you're going to read each item and write the missing words.

b. **Remember—the first sound of each missing word is already written in the blank.**

END OF LESSON 81

swam far, far away. arf was
not happy now.

then a big, big fish that līked
to ēat sharks swam up to the
other sharks.

"help, help," they yelled.
but the big fish was
swimming after them very fast.

stop

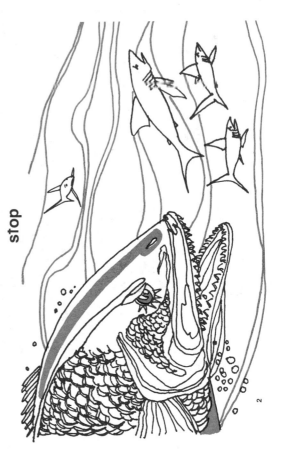

arf the shark

arf was a barking shark. arf
was a little shark, but shē had a
big bark that māde the other fish
swim away.

a shark swam up to arf and
said, "you are a shark. let's plāy."

arf was happy. "arf, arf,"
shē said. and the other shark
swam far, far away. arf was
not happy now.

another shark swam up to
arf. "you are a shark," hē said.
"let's plāy."

arf was happy. "arf, arf,"
shē said. and the other shark

stōry Ītems

1. arf was a barkīng ▒▒▒▒▒ .

● card   ● shark   ● farm

2. a big ▒▒▒▒▒ swam up to the other sharks.

● fish   ● fin   ● fan

shē is in a car.

shē is in a car.

---

h — — — — —

w — — — — —

v — — — — —

n — — — — —

u — — — — —

m — — — — —

rēadīng

a boy āte cāke.

hē got sick.

1. a ▒▒▒▒▒ āte cāke.

● man   ● boy   ● girl

2. hē got ▒▒▒▒▒ .

● sick   ● sad   ● wet

---

1. this **m** _____ is ōld.

2. hē has a **r** _____ .

1. the **b** _____ is in the trēē.

2. the **p** _____ is in the trēē.

Placement Test Scoring Sheet for Reading Mastery

Student's Name _____ Date _____

Circle 1 point or 2 points if the student answers correctly.

PART 1			
Task 1	step b	0	1 point
	step c	0	1 point
Task 2	step b	0	1 point
		0	1 point
		0	1 point
		0	1 point
		0	1 point
	step d	0	1 point
		0	1 point
		0	1 point
		0	1 point
		0	1 point
Task 3	step b	0	2 points
	step c	0	2 points
Task 4	step b	0	2 points
	step d	0	2 points

Total Points ☐

PART 2			
Task 1	step a	0	2 points
	step b	0	2 points
Task 2	step b	0	1 point
		0	1 point
	step c	0	1 point
		0	1 point
	step d	0	1 point
		0	1 point

Total Points ☐

Number of Points	Start at:
0-7	Reading Mastery I, lesson 11
8-10	If possible, should be placed in Reading Mastery: Fast Cycle I.

Number of Points	Start At:
0-14	Reading Mastery I, lesson 1
15-18	Reading Mastery I, lesson 11 (Circle the lesson)
19-20	Continue testing in part 2. (Check box) ☐

Rate and Accuracy Chart

Name	54	55	57	60	62	65	67	72	75	77	86	90	95	103	111	116	121	129	134	139	144	149	153	160	165	170

Reading Vocabulary Word List

This list includes only those words that are introduced in Reading Vocabulary. Additional words are used in the stories and take homes. The number following each word refers to the lesson in which the word first appears in Reading Vocabulary.

able 139
about 97
across 142
afraid 127
after 78
again 106
agreed 146
air 140
Alaska 150
alive 155
all 84
alligator 136
almost 95
alone 138
along 132
also 89
always 89
am 10
an 21
and 32
angry 165
animal 129
another 81
answer 114
answered 137
ant 33
any 90
anybody 119
anyhow 133
anyone 101
anything 117
anywhere 166
appear 135
appeared 141
appears 139
apple 136
are 56
arf 81
arm 57
around 119
arrows 170
as 123
asked 83
at 22
ate 27
away 81

babies 164
baby 119
back 64
bags 119
bald 164
ball 84
balls 93
banana 159
bananas 161
bank 140
banking 139
bark 168
barked 82
barking 81
barn 75
be 63
beach 137
bead 129
bean 134
beat 138
became 115
because 92
become 146
bed 64
been 103
before 100
began 107
behind 101
being 140
believe 142
believed 143
belong 150
bent 85
best 107
bet 88
better 72
bide 138
big 63
bigger 102
biggest 128
bin 133
bird 140
bit 63
bite 126
biter 155
bites 132
biting 149

bitter 155
blanks 144
blew 165
blushed 140
bode 130
bones 83
bong 154
boo 127
book 76
books 82
boss 121
bottles 136
bottom 103
bout 96
box 71
boy 67
branch 151
breathe 169
broke 114
broken 143
broom 78
brother 68
brown 157
brush 73
brushed 73
bug 62
bugs 63
bumpy 135
bunch 138
bus 64
bust 138
but 68
button 99
buying 112

cake 56
call 84
called 87
calling 88
cam 104
came 92
can 23
candy 88
cane 103
caned 122
canes 143
canned 122

canner 125
cannot 87
cans 143
can't 87
cap 102
cape 102
caped 131
capped 131
car 56
card 69
care 108
careful 102
Carla 138
Carmen 97
carry 119
cars 57
cash 126
cast 128
castle 128
casts 134
cat 22
cats 65
cave 152
caves 58
chair 157
charm 100
chasing 153
cheek 118
cheeks 152
cheer 92
cheered 92
cheering 92
cheese 125
chicken 151
children 97
China 150
chip 72
chop 160
chunk 158
chunks 88
circle 82
city 139
clapped 150
class 148
clean 104
close 111
closed 111
closer 142
clothes 156
cloud 95
clouds 99
coat 54
cold 166
colder 110
color 154

come 70
coming 100
con 111
cone 111
coned 138
cones 151
conned 111
cons 151
continued 113
cooked 81
cool 111
cop 54
cope 133
copper 142
corn 61
could 89
couldn't 91
cow 45
crash 116
crashed 116
cream 111
cried 86
croak 155
crooks 112
cross 102
crow 151
crump 156
crying 102
cut 63

dad 67
Dan 21
dance 156
dancing 158
dare 146
dark 114
darn 169
dart 132
day 73
dear 19
deep 97
deepest 156
deer 68
did 42
didn't 116
dig 113
dim 111
dime 83
dimes 114
dimmed 137
dimmer 137
diner 120
dinner 91
dirty 104
disappear 136

disappeared 162
disappears 142
dish 42
dive 65
do 59
does 104
doesn't 133
dog 55
doing 66
done 109
don't 87
door 101
doors 113
down 55
dream 86
dreaming 86
dress 130
dresses 130
drink 111
dropped 86
duckling 151
dug 85
dumped 123
dusty 158

each 57
eagle 71
ear 12
ears 42
easiest 166
easy 139
eat 34
eaten 161
eating 62
eight 163
either 74
elephant 109
elf 102
else 107
even 88
ever 89
Everest 168
every 89
everybody 109
everything 157
eyes 99

face 140
fact 142
fall 94
falling 93
fan 23
far 82
farm 57
farmer 134

fast 79
fat 22
father 99
fatter 78
fear 18
feed 14
feel 47
feet 25
fell 75
felt 91
few 144
fig 35
fight 146
figure 166
filed 161
filled 76
fin 93
find 67
fine 83
fingers 148
fire 111
first 125
fish 45
fishing 65
fit 25
fixed 119
fixes 125
flame 152
flash 132
flew 132
flies 138
flip 144
flipped 144
flipping 145
float 129
floated 129
floating 132
flock 155
floor 85
flow 142
flowed 146
flower 133
fly 76
flying 108
fog 55
folded 139
fool 125
football 88
footprint 151
for 49
forest 140
forget 139
forgot 163
formed 142
forward 158

found 101
four 163
fox 71
frog 128
from 78
front 145
full 102
fun 31
funny 81

game 92
games 127
gaped 152
gapped 152
gas 113
gate 47
gave 51
genie 135
genies 137
get 60
getting 63
ghost 127
girl 58
give 51
giving 111
glad 98
glass 143
go 50
goat 53
goes 86
going 62
gold 76
gone 159
good 114
got 42
grabbed 100
grape 160
grass 98
grasshopper 156
green 128
grew 132
ground 99
grown 147

had 50
hadn't 159
hair 150
hall 84
hand 37
handed 114
handle 162
handsome 151
hanging 100
happen 143
happened 113

happy 89
hard 85
hardest 150
has 38
hasn't 159
hat 35
hate 35
hated 163
hater 140
hatter 140
have 50
haven't 141
having 66
he 29
head 80
heap 127
hear 113
hears 42
heave 116
heaved 132
heel 137
held 95
help 81
helped 81
her 68
here 61
here's 170
herself 99
he'll 132
he's 147
hid 104
hide 104
hill 44
him 48
himself 91
his 29
hit 29
hitting 71
hold 52
holding 105
hole 86
holes 114
home 59
hop 70
hope 86
hoped 125
hoper 133
hoping 126
hopped 115
hopper 133
hopping 126
horse 75
horses 127
hot 29
hotter 151

hounds 100
house 97
how 45
howling 129
hug 48
hugged 170
hugs 52
human 145
hungry 147
hunt 68
hunting 68
hut 39

ice 111
icebox 138
idea 167
if 15
impossible 145
in 21
inside 87
instant 147
into 104
is 18
it 19
it's 145
I'll 85
I'm 103
I've 120

jail 122
jailer 122
Japan 150
Jean 156
jerk 165
job 108
joke 152
jump 74
jumped 78
junk 138
just 95

keep 106
kept 91
key 121
kick 49
kicked 90
kim 60
kind 139
king 60
kiss 48
kissed 89
kit 107
kite 107
kites 107
kitten 51

knew 158
knock 131
knocked 132
know 126
known 148

lake 48
land 37
last 85
late 36
laugh 127
laughed 130
laughing 128
lead 131
leaf 130
leave 83
leaves 125
left 84
let 60
letter 169
let's 94
lick 36
licked 170
licking 170
licks 44
lid 39
lie 103
lied 167
lies 138
life 80
lift 61
lifted 157
light 154
like 64
liked 81
likes 84
listen 155
little 40
lived 90
lock 37
log 55
long 118
longer 118
longest 160
look 80
looked 78
looking 88
looks 82
loop 168
lots 50
loud 95
love 68
loved 74
lunch 153
lying 112

mad 16
made 33
magic 99
mail 38
make 107
makes 107
making 107
mall 85
mammal 159
man 24
many 102
Marta Flores 145
master 135
masters 149
matter 156
maybe 135
me 11
meal 83
mean 35
meaner 131
meanest 129
meets 86
melt 138
men 61
mess 115
met 60
metal 165
middle 139
might 134
miles 115
mitt 30
mixed 108
mole 85
mom 45
monkey 165
monster 128
moo 97
mooing 98
moon 72
mop 54
mope 112
moped 120
moping 119
mopped 113
mopper 113
mopping 114
more 93
most 120
mother 68
mountain 99
mouse 97
mouth 111
move 150
much 88
mud 33

muddy 162
must 73
my 76
myself 130

nail 38
nailed 120
name 36
named 83
near 92
neat 24
need 53
needed 95
never 73
new 128
next 121
nice 151
night 127
nine 122
ninety 122
no 48
nobody 118
none 137
nose 49
not 24
note 92
noted 123
notes 122
nothing 117
now 44
nut 32
nuts 50

oak 122
obey 148
of 50
off 152
oh 86
old 49
on 25
once 99
one 83
only 100
open 100
opened 101
or 49
other 68
Ott 136
ouch 100
our 97
out 95
outside 110
over 71

packed 121
page 158
paint 61
pan 105
pane 105
panes 134
pans 134
paper 107
park 109
parked 116
part 88
parting 144
parts 107
party 86
pass 91
passed 109
past 95
pat 61
path 158
paths 159
patted 149
pay 83
peach 137
peaches 137
peek 135
peevish 156
people 127
person 145
pet 61
petted 97
phone 150
pick 96
picked 86
picks 80
pile 72
piles 137
pine 122
pined 121
pink 158
pinned 121
place 149
plan 112
plane 144
planed 144
planer 145
planing 147
planned 144
planner 145
planning 128
plant 121
planted 123
planting 124
plants 121
plate 132
play 90

played 87
player 93
playing 84
plays 82
please 87
plop 132
pond 64
poof 140
pool 74
poorest 140
popped 158
pot 56
pots 59
pouch 99
pow 115
pretty 170
prince 156
proud 122
puff 136
pulled 154
puppy 170
put 90

rabbit 66
rag 35
rain 36
rake 47
ram 11
rammed 132
ran 21
rat 23
rate 27
rather 165
rats 48
reached 103
read 14
reading 84
ready 93
real 130
really 109
red 67
remember 139
remembering 159
rest 100
resting 142
rich 104
richest 145
rid 162
riding 75
right 123
ring 149
roared 129
robbed 129
robed 129
rock 23

rocks 49
rocky 159
rod 90
rode 90
rolled 135
rolling 86
rome 139
roots 153
round 104
rubbed 104
rubs 136
rug 37
rugs 52
rule 156
rules 161
run 31
runner 94
running 117
runs 42
rush 150

sack 28
sacks 43
sad 12
said 43
sail 38
salt 85
Sam 26
same 66
sand 36
sat 31
save 50
saved 98
saves 58
saw 85
say 113
saying 113
says 75
scare 127
scared 155
school 109
score 90
scored 92
scores 93
scream 133
screamed 143
seat 58
see 10
seed 12
seem 13
seems 122
seen 68
send 121
sent 69
setting 103

shack 41
shade 144
shark 81
sharks 82
sharp 108
shave 52
she 40
sheep 155
shell 152
she'd 147
she'll 168
shine 77
shining 151
ship 59
shirt 156
shoes 156
shoot 113
shop 70
shopping 70
shore 135
short 149
shot 46
shots 61
should 87
shouldn't 92
shout 95
shouted 98
show 80
showed 149
shut 43
shy 134
sick 25
Sid 120
side 83
silly 87
simple 146
sing 87
sip 134
sit 19
site 103
sitting 71
six 77
sixteen 157
slammed 100
sleep 62
sleeping 71
sleepy 160
slept 156
slid 66
slide 66
slider 166
sliding 65
slipped 78
slop 123
slope 123

slow 79
slowly 101
sly 111
small 84
smart 126
smarter 148
smartest 148
smash 138
smile 77
smiled 77
smiles 115
smiling 134
smoke 136
snake 134
snap 153
snapped 148
sneak 153
sneaking 157
sneaky 154
snow 110
so 50
sock 28
socks 49
soft 161
some 70
somebody 112
someday 166
someone 141
something 104
sometimes 127
soon 73
sorry 108
sound 99
sounded 139
sounds 98
space 156
spank 143
spanking 139
spell 127
spells 132
spend 149
spent 125
spin 140
spitting 146
splash 146
splat 142
spot 83
spotted 85
spring 167
squeak 169
stairs 113
stall 85
stand 75
standing 120
stands 79

star 96
stare 145
stared 168
start 85
started 86
starting 97
stay 85
stayed 105
stays 129
steep 99
step 138
stepped 154
steps 79
stick 143
sticks 121
stones 126
stood 145
stool 153
stop 70
stopped 93
store 74
storm 135
story 83
strange 136
stream 127
streaming 141
street 83
string 126
striped 161
stripes 163
strong 153
stuck 110
suddenly 137
sun 31
super 112
swam 81
swimming 81
swims 82
swing 123
swinging 157
swung 124

table 90
tail 43
take 50
taken 150
takes 137
taking 148
talk 64
talked 72
talking 65
tall 85
taller 88
tallest 160
tame 126

tap 114
tape 115
taped 119
taper 168
tapped 114
tapper 168
tapping 125
tar 56
teach 57
teacher 75
teaches 125
team 92
tear 20
tears 44
teeth 49
tell 66
telling 132
tent 108
test 137
than 72
thank 89
thanked 119
that 21
the 17
their 154
them 65
themselves 131
then 61
there 60
these 83
they 67
they'll 166
they've 150
thing 107
things 79
think 91
thinking 88
third 161
this 27
those 49
thousand 101
thousands 139
three 114
through 142
throw 117
thud 145
thunder 115
tickle 129
tickled 159
tiger 78
Tim 110
time 66
timer 170
times 114
tin 24

tired 103
to 52
toad 129
toadstool 153
today 149
toe 151
toenail 152
tonight 156
took 80
tooth 77
top 54
tops 59
tore 74
tossed 123
touch 77
touched 101
touching 89
town 92
toy 70
trained 150
trapper 164
tree 78
trick 112
tricks 127
tried 91
tries 160
truck 119
true 146
try 92
trying 112
tug 76
turn 129
turned 128
turtle 151
two 114

under 78
understand 166
until 152
up 61
us 33
used 154
using 160
U.S. 168

van 150
vane 150
very 84

vine 160
vow 148
vows 149

wait 126
waited 140
walk 64

walked 72
walking 122
wall 95
walls 116
Walter 91
Walter's 93
want 84
wanted 89
wants 96
warm 165
warmer 167
was 46
watch 155
watched 128
water 146
waved 139
waves 58
we 38
wear 151
weed 151
week 89
well 83
went 60
were 87
wet 60
we're 141
we've 147
whale 166
what 83
wheels 167
when 78
where 77
which 141
while 122
white 77
who 97
why 77
wife 80
will 39
win 44
window 110
windows 143
winter 166
wiped 149
wise 142
wish 44
wished 141
wishes 135

wishing 110
with 43
wizard 156
woke 103
wolf 155
wolves 155
woman 114

wonder 162
wonderful 144
won't 108
wood 108
wooden 160
woods 112
woof 169
word 90
words 121
work 106
worked 108
works 131
world 151
would 87
wouldn't 91

yard 91
year 102
years 139
yelled 78
yelling 124
yellow 104
yes 67
yet 144
you 68
your 75
yourself 149
you'll 163
you're 133
you've 150

Independent Reading List

The following books are suggested for independent student reading. Present the books to your children at any time after they have completed the specified lessons in Reading Mastery: Fast Cycle.

The ISBN numbers are for library or reinforced-binding editions, when available. Many of the books are also available in paperback.

Lesson

75 **Have You Seen My Cat?** Eric Carle. ISBN: 0-531-02552-7. Picture Book Studio. 94 words. When a boy's cat disappears, his search leads him to many other cats, but none are his cat. In the end, a man and woman tell him where his cat is.

75 **Look What I Can Do.** Jose Aruego. Out of Print.* Scribner. 19 words. One water buffalo shows off, and a second water buffalo imitates each action. After they become exhausted, a third water buffalo appears and begins to show what it can do. The other two sit on the showoff buffalo.

80 **Snake In, Snake Out.** Linda Banchek. ISBN: 0-690-03853-4. Harper-Row. 38 words. A lady's pet snake and parrot perform playful tricks. The text uses the words **in, out, on, up, over, off, down,** and **under** to describe where the snake is.

83 **We Hide, You Seek.** Jose Aruego & Ariane Dewey. ISBN: 0-688-84201-1. Greenwillow. 29 words. A nearsighted rhino who is playing a game of hide-and-seek accidentally finds the other animals who are hiding by stepping on them or startling them. Then the rhino hides in a unique hiding place. The other animals cannot find the rhino because the rhino hides in a group of other rhinos.

84 **If At First . . .** Sandra Boynton. ISBN: 0-316-10487-6. Little. 28 words. A persistent mouse tries, tries, and tries again to coax a lazy elephant up a hill.

84 **The Monkey and the Bee.** Leland Jacobs. Out of Print. Western Pub. 230 words. A curious animal observes a tree with a monkey in it. A bee bothers the monkey, who hits the bee. The angered bee bites the monkey. Then the bee chases the observer as the monkey laughs.

87 **I Love You, Dear Dragon.** Margaret Hillert. ISBN: 0-8136-5023-2. Modern Curr. 275 words. A dragon accompanies a boy to school, makes valentines with him, and sits with him when the boy's father reads stories. The boy loves dear dragon.

88 **I Can Read.** Dick Bruna. ISBN: 0-8431-1542-4. Price Stern. 55 words. A little girl can read words describing herself and her family.

91 **If All the Seas Were One Sea.** Janina Domanska. ISBN: 0-02-732540-7. Macmillan. 89 words. The story suggests what would happen if all trees became one tree, if all axes were made into one ax, and if all people were combined to make one person. If all the seas were one sea, what a great sea that would be.

94 **The School.** John Burningham. ISBN: 0-690-00903-8. Harper-Row. 27 words. The experiences that a boy has at his school include: reading, writing, painting pictures, playing games, and making friends.

95 **How Do I Put It On?** Shigeo Watanabe. ISBN: 0-399-20761-9. Philomel. 100 words. A bear has difficulty dressing. After putting the clothes on the wrong body parts, the bear finally puts the clothes on properly—and with no help.

96 **Blue Sea.** Robert Kalan. ISBN: 0-688-84184-8. Greenwillow. 75 words. Bigger fish chase smaller fish through holes. The only fish that gets through the smallest hole is the littlest fish.

102 **Find the Cat.** Elaine Livermore. ISBN: 0-395-14756-5. Houghton Mifflin. 105 words. A dog searches for an elusive cat that has a bone and hides in different parts of the house. Pictures show some of the cat's intriguing hiding places.

*Some books are included although they are out of print because they are commonly found in school libraries.

103 **Inside Outside Upside Down.** Stanley Berenstain & Janice Berenstain. ISBN: 0-394-91142-3. Random. 69 words. A curious animal climbs into a box. The animal goes to town upside-down, but the box falls off the truck right-side-up in front of the animal's home.

104 **A Good Day, a Good Night.** Cindy Wheeler. ISBN: 0-397-31901-0 Harper-Row. 80 words. Marmalade is a cat who has a good day and a good night. Marmalade gets fresh milk from the cow and has fun with a robin, a lightning bug, a bat, and a rabbit. At night, a friendly moon smiles at them.

106 **Green Eggs & Ham.** Dr. Seuss. ISBN: 0-394-90016-2. Beginner Books. 812 words. Sam-I-Am repeatedly offers a character wearing a black hat green eggs and ham, but the character refuses to eat them until the end of the story. The character then discovers that green eggs and ham are good.

107 **Go, Dog, Go!** Philip D. Eastman. ISBN: 0-394-90020-0. Beginner Books. 518 words. Dogs of various shapes, colors, and sizes have a series of adventures in cars, on boats, and in trees.

107 **The Farmer in the Dell.** Diane Zuromskis. ISBN: 0-316-98889-8. Little. 159 words. The lyrics from the familiar song are combined with pictures.

107 **Mine's the Best.** Crosby N. Bonsall. ISBN: 0-06-020578-4. Harper-Row. 107 words. Two boys have balloons at the beach. Each boy argues that his balloon is the best. As the boys argue, the balloons deflate. Then somebody comes along the beach with bundles of fully-inflated balloons.

107 **The Snow.** John Burningham. ISBN: 0-690-00905-4. Harper-Row. 47 words. After a snowfall, a boy and his mother roll a snowball, build a snowman, and play with a sled. When the boy loses his mitten, they go inside, but he hopes the snow will be there tomorrow.

107 **The Rabbit.** John Burningham. ISBN: 0-690-00907-0. Harper-Row. 61 words. A boy likes to feed his pet rabbit dandelions. Sometimes the rabbit gets out of its cage. It likes to hop around in the garden, but it eats plants. The boy has to catch it and return it to its cage.

107 **Yellow Yellow.** Frank Asch. Out of Print. McGraw. 100 words. A boy finds a yellow hard hat that he wears, floats a cat in, stands on, and put plants in. But the owner comes along and takes the hat back. Soon, however, the boy has a new hat—a paper hat that he made and decorated.

107 **One Little Kitten.** Tana Hoban. ISBN: 0-688-84222-4. Greenwillow. 53 words. A little kitten discovers exciting places to play and hide. Photographs show the kitten's activities.

107 **Lollipop.** Wendy Watson. ISBN: 0-690-00768-X. Harper-Row. 150 words. A bunny's mother refuses to give him a lollipop, so the bunny goes to a store, where nobody notices him. He falls asleep; returns home late; receives a spanking, a kiss, and then a lollipop.

107 **The Carrot Seed.** Ruth Krauss. ISBN: 0-06-023350-6. Harper-Row. 101 words. A boy plants a carrot seed. Members of his family tell the boy that the seed will not grow. But it does grow—into a gigantic carrot.

107 **New Dog Next Door.** Elizabeth Bridgman. Out of Print. Harper-Row. 81 words. The dog next door adopts a boy and his family. The dog does nice things for the boy and his family.

107 **Whose Mouse Are You?** Robert Kraus. ISBN: 0-02-751190-1. Macmillan. 108 words. A lonely mouse liberates its mother from inside a cat, its father from inside a trap, and its sister from a mountaintop. After these heroic efforts, the mouse has a family again, including something new—a baby brother mouse.

107 **The Friend.** John Burningham. ISBN: 0-690-01274-8. Harper-Row. 47 words. A boy tells about his relationship with his friend Arthur. The boys have a lot of fun playing, but when they fight, Arthur goes home and the boy finds interim friends to play with. Arthur remains the best friend, however.

107 **Three Little Kittens Lost Their Mittens.**
Elaine Livermore. ISBN: 0-395-28379-5.
Houghton Mifflin. 95 words. Three kittens
each lose mittens while doing such things as
eating ice cream, reading books, sliding, and
swinging. The mother cat tells the kittens that
they will have no pie until they have found
their mittens, which are hidden in the pictures.

107 **Brown Bear, Brown Bear, What Do You See?**
Bill Martin, Jr. ISBN: 0-03-064164-0. H. Holt.
258 words. Brown bear sees an animal that is
looking at brown bear. That animal in turn
sees another animal who is looking at that
animal. The chain continues through nine
animals.

109 **Wake Up, Jeremiah.** Ronald Himler. ISBN:
0-06-022324-3. Harper-Row. 87 words. At
dawn a boy hurries to dress and follows *it*—on
the stairs, across the grass, and to the top of
the hill. There he sees *it*—the sun. He rushes
home to wake his parents and share the new
day.

110 **Home For a Bunny.** Margaret W. Brown.
ISBN: 0-307-10388-9. Western. 357 words. A
bunny looks for a home in a lot of places
before finding the right home, a hole occupied
by another bunny.

111 **Who Took the Farmer's Hat?** Joan L. Nodset.
ISBN: 0-06-024566-2. Harper-Row. 350 words.
The wind carries the farmer's old brown hat
on a journey that ends when the hat becomes
a bird's nest. The farmer follows the hat's
journey, but when he sees that it is being used
as a nest, he decides to buy a new brown hat.

112 **A Kiss For Little Bear.** Else H. Minarik.
ISBN: 0-06-44050-8, Trophy. Harper-Row. 303
words. Grandmother bear is delighted with the
picture Little Bear has made for her and sends
a kiss back to him by pony express—through
several animals. The kiss almost gets lost.

114 **What Have I Got?** Mike McClintock. ISBN:
0-06-024141-1. Harper-Row. 238 words.
Exciting things happen to a boy whose pockets
are filled with objects, including a ball, a
penny, a car, and a hook. He imagines the
things he can do with his possessions—get
candy with the penny, hit a home run with the
ball, go far in his toy car, and catch a fish with
his hook.

116 **Hop on Pop.** Dr. Seuss. ISBN: 0-394-90029-4.
Beginner Books. 383 words. Some characters
have adventures sitting on hats, sitting on a
cactus, and playing ball on a wall. Others find
out that they should not hop on pop.

Scope and Sequence Chart

SOUNDS AND LETTER NAMES

Sounds	1 ———————————— 89
Sound Combinations (Diphthongs and Digraphs)	81 ———————————— 170
Letter Names—Vowels	90–100
Letter Names—Consonants	114–117
Alphabetical Order	114–117
Capital Letters	118–125

PRONUNCIATION

1 ——— 21

SEQUENCING GAMES

1–3

BLENDING

Say the Sounds	1–2
Say It Fast	1–6
Say the Sounds—Say It Fast	1 ——— 16
Sounds—Say It Fast	2–8
Say It Fast—Rhyming	3–7
Sound Out	4–12
Rhyming	8–15

READING VOCABULARY

Sounding Out Words — 10 ———————— 113

Reading the Fast Way — 27 ———————————— 170

Word Attack Skills

Regular Words	10 ———————————— 170
Rhyming Words	15 ——————— 80
Words Beginning with Stop Sounds	29 ——— 42
Irregular Words	43 ———————————— 170
Word Build-ups	66 ——— 78
Word Parts	81 ———————————— 170
Final-e Rule	97 ——— 111
Spelling by Letter Names	117 ———————— 170

Note: The skills shown on the Scope and Sequence Chart reflect only their structured presentation, not their continued use.

STORY READING—DECODING

Skill	Range
Sounding Out Words	17 — 53
Reading the Fast Way	36 — 170
Rate-and-Accuracy Checkouts	54 — 170
Related Story-Reading Skills	
Word Finding	26 — 42
Period Finding	43
Sentence Saying	43 — 53
Quotation Finding	46–53
Question Mark Finding	48–50
Reading the Title	57–59

STORY READING— COMPREHENSION

Skill	Range
Picture Questions	17 — 170
Story Questions—Oral	36 — 170
Story Questions—Written	66 — 170
Related Comprehension Skills	
Read the Items	76 — 89 112–125
Rule Review	157–170

TAKE-HOME EXERCISES

Skill	Range
Say It Fast	1–4
Sound Writing	1 — 83
Cross-Out Games	1 — 65
Picture Completion	1 — 16
Sound Out	2 — 12
Pair Relations	5 — 71
Matching	10 — 59
Reading Vocabulary	13–16
Sentence and Story Copying	17 — 97
Reading Comprehension	60 — 170
Story Items	66 — 170
Picture Comprehension	72 — 83
Following Instructions	83 — 144
Story-Picture Items	107 — 125
Picture Deductions	126 — 157
Story-Items Review	127 — 157
Written Deductions	147 — 170
Factual Information Passages	151 — 170

Pronunciation Guide

Symbol	Pronounced	As in	Voiced or Unvoiced*	Introduced in Lesson
a	aaa	and	v	1
m	mmm	ram	v	1
s	sss	bus	uv	3
ē	ēēē	eat	v	4
r	rrr	bar	v	6
d	d	mad	v	9
f	fff	stuff	uv	11
i	iii	if	v	13
th	ththth	this and bathe (not thing)	v	15
t	t	cat	uv	17
n	nnn	pan	v	19
c	c	tack	uv	21
o	ooo	ox	v	23
ā	āāā	ate	v	26
h	h	hat	uv	28
u	uuu	under	v	30
g	g	tag	v	33
l	lll	pal	v	35
w	www	wow	v	37
sh	shshsh	wish	uv	39

Symbol	Pronounced	As in	Voiced or Unvoiced	Introduced in Lesson
I	(the word I)		v	43
k	k	tack	uv	45
ō	ōōō	over	v	48
v	vvv	love	v	50
p	p	sap	uv	54
ch	ch	touch	uv	57
e	eee	end	v	59
b	b	grab	v	61
ing	iiing	sing	v	62
ī	īīī	ice	v	64
y	yyy	yard	v	66
er	urrr	brother	v	67
x	ksss	ox	uv	70
oo	oooooo	moon (not look)	v	71
J	j	judge	v	72
ȳ	īīī	my	v	75
wh	www or wh	why	v or uv	76
qu	kwww (or koo)	quick	v	77
z	zzz	buzz	v	78
ū	ūūū	use	v	80

*Voiced sounds are sounds you make by vibrating your vocal chords. You do not use your vocal chords for unvoiced sounds—you use air only. To feel the difference between voiced and unvoiced sounds, hold your throat lightly and say the sound *vvv*. You will feel your vocal chords vibrating. Then, without pausing, change the sound to *fff*. The vibrations will stop. The only difference between the sounds is that the *vvv* is voiced and the *fff* is not.

Sound Combinations, Digraphs, and Diphthongs

al	er	sh
ar	ing	th
ch	oo	wh
ea	ou	
ee	qu	